HATE'S RECOMPENSE

Hate's Recompense

by Joseph Gibson

To my brother and sister, R. John Gibson and Judy Voss—life-long warriors against hate.

CHAPTER 1

CALIFORNIA SENATOR ALEJANDRA TRUJILLO rode in the backseat of her Uber from her condo in Venice to the LA Civic Center. She was on her way to speak at the final rally for the vote against Sentinel tomorrow. She smiled at the thousands of protestors in the streets and rolled down her window to wave as she approached the downtown area.

"La Serpiente!" came from her followers as they saw who it was.

As she waved to the crowds, she showed pictures of the scene to her fifteen-year-old daughter, Maria, the only love of her life after her husband had been killed in Guatemala sixteen months and five days ago.

"I don't like you being down there without some kind of protection," Maria said. "Trying to save taxpayer money by riding in Ubers is not smart in a situation like that."

"You are such a mother hen," Aleja responded. "I'm supposed to be the mother in this family."

"Dammit, Momma, you're not a SEAL or a cop anymore. You've got lots of enemies and plenty of people who think you're unqualified for your job. The Nationalists would love to see you dead."

Aleja was about to respond when a series of explosions captured her attention. Screams filled the air, and the crowds broke in all directions. "Gotta go, honey," she said.

"Turn around and get the hell out of there!" Maria cried.

"I've got my gun. I am still a certified peace officer and always will be. I took an oath to maintain the peace, and that's what I will do."

"Call for backup right now!"

"Too late for that," Aleja came back. "We're blocked in from behind."

A group of four men in black hoods suddenly emerged from the crowd and approached the Uber, two on each side. "Lock the doors and get down!" she called to her driver.

Seeing that the men were armed with P9 machine guns, she pulled her Sig Sauer Mk.25 from her shoulder pack and squeezed off a handful of rounds. They apparently weren't expecting her to shoot first, and the two on the left fell to her burst before they could get a shot off. But when she moved to the other side of the backseat to face the other two attackers, the reception was different. One of them rolled something under the SUV, then both men blasted out her windows with their machine guns. An explosion sent her tumbling into the front seat, where the driver had been thrown into his steering wheel and knocked out. Flames shot up through holes in the floorboards, making Aleja gag on the smoke.

She slid the driver over, unlocked the doors, and exited the driver's side. Rolling onto the pavement, she stayed on her belly to evade the fifty-round, close-range assault guns. Her only line of sight was under the car, and she opened fire, hitting one of her attackers in the leg and the other in the foot. Their recoil gave her just enough time to come to her feet and empty her clip into them over the front hood. She quickly reloaded with the spare clip in her shoulder pack, rushed around to the passenger side, and pulled the driver out just as the gas tank exploded. They both were blown off their feet and sent flying through the air.

Momentarily dazed by the explosion and unable to hear, she staggered to her feet and dragged the driver away from the blazing truck. She'd lost her gun in the explosion but had no time to go back for it now. She had to get out of there. She prayed she wouldn't have to fight again soon.

CHAPTER 2

BUR MCANTER, CHIEF TECHNOLOGY architect of the Cyber Command Center, sat in his office overlooking the main control floor of the massive top-secret facility. Tonight, he anxiously awaited news from President Kahn about the vote in Congress tomorrow on the adoption of Sentinel, Bur's all-encompassing security shield to protect the nation from cyberattack. Bur had developed the first iteration of Sentinel with Jenks Kennard at Cornell, where they had envisioned the use of artificial intelligence to usher in a new digital age.

Bur had been hired to build Sentinel by General Alex Stanyan of Air Force Intelligence. Bur had accepted Stanyan's offer despite the strong objections of Jenks, who had stayed at Cornell writing extensively about the perils of Sentinel in the wrong hands. Bur had proceeded anyway, primarily because of his political leanings toward President Kahn.

When Kahn had seen the finished product, he had immediately fallen in love with it and signed an executive order to implement it nationwide. News of Sentinel had quickly gotten out, and the Resistance-held House swiftly passed a bill to block the executive order. Now, it was going to the Nationalist-held Senate for a vote. If the Senate failed to support the

House's bill, the executive order would automatically go into effect.

The vote had brought out millions of protestors across the country, including almost the entire state of California. Bur had been nervous for the past two weeks, as he'd seen the pressure the Resistance was putting on Nationalist senators to support their blockage of the executive order. Even though Kahn was confident he could kill the bill in the Senate, Bur had an intuition that something bad was about to happen. Some of the more radical members of the Resistance had mentioned war if Sentinel was passed. Bur had gone to great lengths, expounding the capabilities of Sentinel to prevent all forms of terrorism in the country, and he believed that people would be willing to accept the chip implants Sentinel required to ensure their safety.

Looking up at the main clock of the control center, Bur saw that it was nearly 10:00 p.m., which meant he needed to call his wife and kids before they went to bed. He activated the video-conferencing monitor.

His wife, son, and daughter appeared before him, sitting in their small flat in the Haight-Ashbury District of San Francisco. So different there from here at Eagle's Cliff, six hours north of them on one of the most treacherous stretches of coastline on the Pacific. "Hey, you guys," he called out to them.

"Daddy!" came from Jimmy, his five-year-old son, who was sitting along with his two-year-old sister, Genevieve, on Carmen's lap. Seeing his family made him ache to be with them again. He felt both anger and guilt that it had been over a month since he'd seen them. He recalled that day clearly now. They'd been walking in Golden Gate Park on a brisk Sunday morning under the giant eucalyptus trees. Bur held Jimmy's hand, walking alongside Carmen, who pushed Genevieve in a stroller. They had just played hide-and-seek in the Botanical

Gardens and then skipped rocks across the pond near the Conservatory. Now Jimmy had a new game.

"Bet you I can beat you there," Jimmy had said, pointing to two solitary evergreens across the manicured grounds.

Bur had looked ahead, figuring it was an easy bet. "You're on," he said, shaking hands.

"And Mommy has to join us," the boy said, grinning.

"Oh, I get it. If your mother has to run, too, that means that one of us has to carry the baby. Of course, you knew that would be me."

Jimmy folded his arms across his chest and nodded smugly. "You on or not?"

Bur bent down and swooped Genevieve out of the stroller. "You're on." He lined up Jimmy and Carmen on either side of him while he held Genevieve snugly in his arms. "Get ready, get set, go!"

The four broke into a run, led by their yelping collie, Malcolm. Bur started fast, then tapered off, feigning fatigue, to let Jimmy take over the lead. Malcolm crossed the finish line first, then Jimmy and Carmen. Bur brought up the rear. Puffing hard, he fell to his knees, laughing as he rolled his gleeful daughter onto the grass.

Jimmy ran back and patted Bur's shoulder. "I won, Dad," he gloated. "I snookered you."

Face-to-face with his son, Bur saw how different the boy was than he had been at that age. His dad had been sick and dying. There'd been no joy for him until he'd met Carmen at age sixteen.

"You didn't win," he said, poking Jimmy playfully in the belly. "Malcolm did."

"But I beat you," Jimmy said defiantly, pushing his hand away. "That was the bet."

"Okay, okay," Bur said reluctantly, "but I got distracted by your mother." He eyed her sleek, fit body as she picked up the baby.

"All talk, no action," she said, leaning down over him so that her thick hair fell into his face. He could smell the chocolate on her breath from her one major vice. "You were so far behind me..." He kissed her there on the grass, right in front of his children.

"Stop it," she said, pushing him away teasingly.

He stood up, laughing. "Okay, next game, let's try something I'm really good at."

"Like what?" Jimmy said.

He tackled Jimmy by surprise, pinning him to the ground. "Wrestling."

Carmen pounced on him, trying to push him off Jimmy. "Yeah?" she said. "We aren't afraid of you."

He rolled her and Jimmy over, but she tickled him as he tried to fight her off. Feeling her full breasts against his chest drove him crazy. He finally freed himself and stood up again, locking Carmen and Jimmy in his arms so they couldn't move.

"Guess that shows who's the dad of this family," he said as they struggled to get free. "Since you won three out of four games this morning, son, you get to choose lunch. What's it going to be?"

"Chili dogs!" Jimmy shouted, jumping up and down with delight.

Bur followed the boy and pushed Genevieve in the stroller. Carmen walked beside him with her arm around his waist. "We're going to miss you when you go back to Eagle's Cliff," she said.

"I'll only be gone during the weekdays. You can expect me on your doorstep every Thursday night for dinner and an early turn-in."

She pinched him and purred into his ear. "I'll be waiting."

He stopped and pulled her to him. "I'm going to give you the world, baby, just like we talked about in high school."

"I'll settle for just you," she replied. "I don't care what happens as long as we're together."

"I was thinking maybe another child would be a nice addition to the family."

She poked him in the stomach. "I'm getting too old for that."

"Like hell," he said, inspecting her. "You look terrific. Grrrr."

"Shhh, stop it." She shot a glance at the children.

Bur came out of his daydream at the sound of a chopper landing on the helipad, no doubt coming in from Vandenburg AFB twenty miles to the north. The location of the complex had been carefully selected to coordinate the many satellite launches and clandestine cybersecurity operations planned by the air force under the Kahn administration.

"Hopefully, you've had something decent to eat tonight?" Carmen said to him, smiling on his monitor.

Looking into her deep hazel eyes made him want to pull her in and kiss her. "No such luck. Cigarettes and coffee only. God, I miss you."

"We miss you too, Daddy," Jimmy said. "Genny can walk." He reached over and kissed his little sister sloppily on the cheek.

Bur took a deep breath to keep from trembling. What could have been more important than seeing his little girl walk for the first time?

"What's the news?" Carmen said, handing Genevieve a teddy bear to play with.

"Nothing yet. I know the president is busy trying to solidify opposition to the bill."

"When are you coming home?" she asked nervously.

Bur tried to hide his concern. "Stanyan said the whole team could take the weekend off as a deserved reward, no matter what happens tomorrow in Washington. I'm planning to be home tomorrow night. I can't tell you how much I want to see you."

"Tomorrow night!" Jimmy screamed. "Yeah! Let me tell Malcolm." The little boy scrambled off his mother's lap and lunged for the huge collie, who sat eagerly at the feet of his humans, trying to see Carmen's phone screen. "Daddy's coming home!" Jimmy said to the dog, provoking a vigorous bark.

Carmen laughed and leaned in closer to the camera. "And I want to see you too," she said, puckering her lips and sending him a kiss. "I will have crab pasta and a bottle of Cakebread Chardonnay waiting for you."

"I won't be hungry," he said, mesmerized by her haunting eyes.

"Stop that now." She wrinkled her nose at him. "The kids..."

"Malcolm can watch them while we get reacquainted."

"Now what on earth would people think if they knew you'd let a dog watch your kids while you were reacquainting with your wife?"

"Don't give a damn," Bur replied. "I'd tell them Malcolm is a certified babysitter and I trust him with the lives of my children. Just let anyone watch him with them for two minutes and end of story."

Jimmy had his arms around the big dog's neck. He was unable to keep the beast from covering his face with licks.

The smile left Carmen's face. "You think you have a chance of overriding the House's bill?"

Bur stirred in his chair. "Yes, but I don't like the protests. I am counting on people coming to their senses and understanding that we must have Sentinel to stay safe. But whatever happens, I am coming home, come hell or high water."

The concern left her face, and the smile came back. "It will be good to see you, baby. Can't wait!"

He was about to respond when his boss came in. "Gotta go, honey, see you soon."

Bur turned to meet his boss, General Alexander Stanyan. At six-six and two-seventy-five, the general cut a formidable figure with his closely cropped blond hair, thick blond mustache, and intense blue eyes. In contrast, Bur wore his graying hair long. He had a full gray beard and stood seven inches shorter and fifty pounds lighter. Bur stared at the big man expectantly, knowing how close he was with the president because of his conservative views on public surveillance.

"The president wants to talk to us," Stanyan said.

Bur took in a deep breath to calm himself as Stanyan dialed a number on the secured video-conferencing unit that Bur had just been using. Bur knew it was against policy to use it for personal business, but he carried a certain amount of clout around here that gave him leeway.

"Good evening, gentlemen," the president said sternly, in his deep southern accent.

Bur stiffened at his tone, seeing the coldness in Kahn's husky like blue eyes that seemed so much more prominent now than when he had first met him.

"I have grave news, I am sorry to say. We have intercepted communications that indicate a forthcoming cyberattack on the power grid in Los Angeles within the next twenty-four hours. Dr. McAnter, I want you to leave first thing tomorrow morning for LA to be there to stop it if it does happen."

Bur clenched his fists in rage. "Dammit! I was afraid of this. The Resistance will be to blame if I can't stop it."

"Yes," Kahn agreed, narrowing his wolfen eyes. "But there's nothing we can do now other than curtail the damage."

"Get me down there!" Bur said. "I will stop it and find out who did it. That should finally bring the Resistance over to our side."

"Let us pray so," Kahn said. "I will be in touch with you when you get there."

CHAPTER 3

ALEJA WAS RELIEVED WHEN her Uber driver regained consciousness and was able to walk on his own. She still had to keep her arm around his waist, though, to steady him as they were bumped along in the panicked crowds of men, women, and children. She tried 911 again on her cell phone, but there was no service. All she could do was implore the people to follow her away from the exploding smoke bombs and get out of the area. Many recognized her as she moved and followed her, calling out to her, "La Serpiente."

She emerged onto Fifth Street with several hundred people in her wake, relieved to see that the explosions had not yet hit there. However, there were plenty of young outlaws on the rampage, robbing, raping, and terrorizing. Ahead, she saw a police car. She hurried for it, but then abruptly stopped, seeing two wounded officers on their knees in front of the bullet-ridden car with their hands tied behind their backs. They were surrounded by a gang of teenagers with drawn pistols, taunting them to beg for their lives. She cursed that she'd lost her gun in the SUV explosion.

"Stop!" she shouted, releasing her arm from her Uber driver so she could proceed unhindered. "You're under arrest," she said, approaching them angrily. "Put your guns down and raise your hands in the air."

The bangers recognized her immediately and laughed. "Hey, snake lady," the leader said, "you ain't no cop anymore, you ain't got no gun, and ain't got no backup, so what the fuck you think you gonna to do to stop us? Fuck us to death?" His comment brought a round of laughter from his gang.

"I've put in a call for help," she bluffed. "When my backup comes, they are going to shoot first and ask questions later. If you want to stay alive, put your guns down now."

They all laughed again. "'Cept the phones ain't workin' and we don't hear no sirens," the leader said. "Streets are blocked anyway. Guess you gonna have to fuck us to death after all." His gang cut up again in glee.

Aleja glared at them as they encircled her, staring them down one at a time. The leader put his pistol in her face. "You can start by suckin' me," he said to her, grinning. "Then I'll let my homies try out your tight little ass."

She nodded her head as if she saw someone coming up behind the banger, distracting him just long enough to head-butt him on the point of his chin, sending him backpedaling into the side of the police car. Pouncing on him like a big cat, she grabbed his gun away and got him in a chokehold, using him as a shield against his gang.

One of them raised his pistol and fired at her, but she expertly positioned the leader to take the bullet in his head rather than hers. Still holding him as a shield, she fired off two quick rounds, leveling two of them, which left three still standing.

She pushed the dead leader into the three, distracting them long enough to fire off a burst of additional rounds, bringing down another two. Facing the single banger left, she shot him in his gun hand, bringing him to his knees, groaning in pain. She turned rapidly to the police officers, untied them, and helped them lay on their backs. "What happened?" she asked, doing her best to attend to their wounds.

"We got stalled in the traffic, and they opened fire on us," one of the officers answered. "Thanks for stepping in, Senator; we'd be dead right now if it weren't for you." He reached up to shake her hand.

She got into the car and used the police radio to call for backup but knew it was unlikely that anyone was going to get through. "We'll carry you with us," she said, motioning for some of her group to help her with them.

She and her group started moving again and more people along the way recognized her and fell in behind her, taking up a song from the movie that had been made about her escape from Venezuelan imprisonment. She had no sense of time and little sense of space as they labored through the stalled cars until they arrived at Parker Center, where officers took charge of her group and then led her rapidly to the city's Emergency Command and Communications Center, five stories underground across the street.

The mayor and police chief hurried to greet her. Mayor Tomas Padilla was another key leader of the Resistance. Police Chief Manny Santos was a Nationalist.

"Thank God, you made it," Padilla said, giving her a big hug. As he held her, she began to shake uncontrollably and cough in spasms. Pushing her slightly away so he could look into her eyes, he said, "You were near one of the smoke bombs?"

She nodded, wiping the sweat from her forehead and feeling a massive headache coming on. "Yes, many," she said. "You shouldn't be touching me."

Padilla shook his head. "Everyone in here has already been exposed. We were at the rally when the explosions started. We've all just been vaccinated and given antibiotics. Together, they are supposed to work, even after exposure. The only issue is that the first responder medics are reporting it's something new, perhaps a new strain, moving much faster than any of the anthrax they've ever heard of. You must have inhaled more of the spores than we did. Get her the vaccine and antibiotics!" he hollered.

She felt dizzy now on top of having a headache and was only marginally aware of someone in a white coat giving her two injections. "It may take up to a day for the antibiotics and vaccine to kick in," the woman said. "You need to try to rest."

The deeply embedded training from her days as a SEAL kicked in, and she ignored how she felt, concentrating on her mission. "We have more important things to deal with right now," she said. "Besides the anthrax, what else?" She tried not to look up at the eight-foot concrete ceiling that made her feel like she was in a brightly lit tomb. She'd categorically refused to enter any type of confined spaces after being imprisoned in Venezuela, and even though she'd tried every known remedy to overcome her fears, they still terrorized her. She wanted to break for the elevator and escape, but she sucked in a deep breath and forced her gaze straight ahead.

"We know it started at DWP," Padilla responded, inspecting her closely. "The electricity went out first. Shortly thereafter, the smoke bombs started. We've been able to support our dispatch and field ops from backup generators, but we can't stop the panic. People think we're under attack."

"How many bombs?" she asked.

"At least a hundred," the police chief responded. "Apparently coordinated. The bombings have died down now, though, thank God. Our priorities are treating the victims, like you, and then getting power back up."

"How many people do you think were exposed?" she asked.

Padilla shook his head and pursed his lips. "Thousands. Impossible to know for sure at this point with the streets blocked. At any rate, we know we don't have enough vaccine here in LA to handle all the victims, so we're in contact with Director Shaw of the CDC in Atlanta right now over our emergency response network."

He directed Aleja's attention to a large monitor, where a middle-aged woman with gray hair sat at a table with a dozen men and women in uniform.

Padilla continued, "Director Shaw, we have Senator Trujillo here now, so please continue."

"Good to hear you have been able to get the vaccine and antibiotics, Senator," the director said with a slight southern accent. "Unfortunately, by the time you get your streets cleared and we fly in more vaccine and antibiotics from other parts of the state and the country, we are bound to have many deaths and many seriously sick people. The hospitals and clinics are going to be overrun."

"And without power, the hospitals can only stay on backup generators for so long," Padilla responded. "Not to mention the traffic jams we have everywhere. Looting and assaults are spreading rapidly..."

He was interrupted by an aide. "It's the president," the young man said, pointing to the videoconference monitor into which Kahn had just been patched.

"Have you apprehended any of the anthrax bombers?" Kahn asked, dispensing with any niceties.

"No," the police chief said.

"If you do apprehend any of them, I want you to personally call me, and I will handle them," Kahn replied briskly. "And I don't want any leaks to your news media about what's happening. We are very vulnerable right now, and I don't want wider-scale panic setting in across the country."

Aleja fought through her dizziness to focus on what the president had just said. "Have any other senators or congressmen been attacked directly?"

Mayor Padilla and the police chief looked at her with concern. "You were attacked directly?" Padilla said.

She nodded. "Four men in black hoodies with a bomb, but not a smoke bomb, a real bomb."

"Gangbangers, you think?" the police chief asked.

The event flashed through her mind again, but it was hard for her to hang on to it. "Not with P9s and an IED."

President Kahn came in. "We believe it was foreign agents. That's why I want you to give me any of them you find or anything they left behind. This was well coordinated. Somebody wanted to hurt us and hurt us badly."

Aleja was now starting to pass in and out of lucidity. "You didn't answer my question," she said to the group at large. "Were any other members of Congress attacked? I know that our local congressional members were supposed to have been there for the rally." She moved her gaze to the mayor. "You said you were there. Did you see any of them?"

Padilla shook his head. "I didn't. They may have been attacked too."

"Get ahold of Senator Little Hawk and have him contact the other Resistance leaders," Aleja said to him.

Kahn abruptly cut in and changed the topic. "I'm sending in the Cyber Defense Team to help with the DWP outage. Bur McAnter should be there shortly."

Aleja's mind was not ready for this fast a change of subject. She still wanted to know how the other Resistance leaders were doing, but Padilla had turned his attention to a young woman with short red hair who had just entered the bunker.

"This is Senior IT Director Endicott from the DWP," the mayor said. "She oversees systems there. Director, can you please give us all an update on what you know so far?"

Facing Aleja respectfully, the young woman said, "I'm glad you're safe, Senator. Something has either disabled or destroyed our computer systems. We haven't lost any data as far as we can determine, we just don't have any way to get at it. We'll need to wipe all our servers clean and reload from yesterday's backups."

"Do you know how it happened?" the president asked.

"We're checking now but could use some help. The CCC would be great."

"Do you feel that other city or county systems are at risk?" Aleja asked.

"I don't know. Perhaps," the woman answered.

The mayor said, "DWP's systems are as current as they come in our local governments. If they can be hacked, then we have to presume others could be also."

"Exactly," said the president.

A policewoman rushed into the room and approached the chief. "This tweet just hit the internet."

The chief read the tweet out loud: "You have seen what we can do to your systems and to your people. Reinstate the Nuclear Deal and drop all sanctions against us now, or we will unleash complete hell on your country. Any attempt to attack us in our homeland, or to harm or arrest our people in America, will bring an instant response of total war from us. We are prepared to expand our attacks a thousand times if you do not comply with our demands."

"Iran," the president said angrily. "Those sons of bitches!"

"To your point, Mr. President, let's not jump to conclusions," Padilla said. "It could also be someone wanting us to think it was Iran. We need to trace the source location of the attack."

"The CCC can help with that," the president said testily. "I'm sure Bur McAnter can figure it out."

The name registered immediately with Aleja. "Isn't he the guy who built Sentinel? We are supposed to vote in Congress on the Sentinel funding bill tomorrow, and less than twenty-four hours before, we have a cyberattack and he is assigned to the case?"

"He is the chief architect of the CCC," the president said. "What are you insinuating, Senator?"

"She is suffering from anthrax inhalation." Padilla jumped in to defend her.

"My mind is a little fuzzy right now, but my instincts are still working," Aleja retorted. "I am getting a great big red flag."

"We have no idea who this tweeter is or who he actually represents," the president said. "There are plenty of radicals in Iran and/or Al-Qaeda who are capable of doing this."

Aleja blew out angrily and turned back to the director from the DWP. "How would you classify this attack? Was this ordinary, something that a radical hacker or two could have pulled off?"

"Depends on the hacker," Director Endicott said, "but from what I know of our security systems, this was quite sophisticated. We will need the CCC to comment further."

"Oh yes we do," Aleja replied. "I have all kinds of questions for the famous Dr. McAnter."

CHAPTER 4

A LATE NOVEMBER STORM had delayed Jenks Kennard's trip from Ithaca, New York, to Custer, South Dakota, to meet with Senator Henry Little Hawk. Jenks had spent nearly all day waiting for planes, since there were no direct flights between the two locations, and now he was very tired and hungry. Except for the funerals of his mother and father, he hadn't been back to Custer since he'd left high school. As he drove into the Crazy Horse Memorial complex, he was surprised to find a large, bustling campus, primarily funded by Henry Little Hawk's millions from his career in the NFL and the numerous successful business ventures he had initiated with various Indian tribes. Jenks was met by some very polite Indian students who escorted him to the former studio of Korczak Ziolkowski, the sculptor of the Crazy Horse Monument.

Jenks could see the blazing fire through the window set in the front door and longed to get out of this bone-chilling cold. His hand shook as he knocked, not sure what was about to happen after all these years. The massive ponderosa pine door opened, and Jenks met Henry's powerful black eyes with a mix of fear and surprise. Henry had not changed in the twenty years since Jenks had last seen him. Six-two, two forty-five, thick black hair, meticulously shaven face. Jenks's parents had always said it was hard to tell the age of an Indian, and Jenks now agreed. Henry was forty, Jenks knew for a fact, but he could easily pass for someone in his early thirties.

"Come in and get warm," Henry said, extending his hand.

Jenks reached out with his left and only hand. Henry's grip had not changed a bit over the years—still as strong as ever.

"We've got a lot of catching up to do," Henry said, "but first let me take your coat and get you some hot coffee and some food."

"That sounds good," Jenks responded as Henry motioned him to a huge pine chair covered by a black bearskin. Jenks willingly took the hot coffee Henry offered.

Now from the other side of the room, Madelena entered. At the sight of her, Jenks dropped his coffee cup onto the thick fur rug. He reached down to pick up his cup and met her face-to-face as she bent to help him.

"Good to see you, Jenks," she said, giving him a big hug. She was wearing a red V-neck sweater and faded red jeans. The last time he'd seen her, she was a skinny high school freshman. Now she was a fully grown woman with perfectly placed cheekbones, mesmerizing black eyes, pronounced garnet lips, and long ebony hair. She sat down in another of the bearskin seats next to Jenks and held his hand. Glancing first at her brother and back to him, she said, "Henry and I have made peace. Now it's time for the three of us to heal."

Jenks stared at her, shocked. "You are so different than the girl I knew in high school."

She let go of his hand. "I've grown up, Jenks," she said. "I've changed. We've all changed. You are no longer the super nerd of Custer High School."

"What have you been doing for the last twenty years?" Jenks continued to stare at her.

Madelena narrowed her eyes. "When I found out that our mother had killed herself after the county gave us to Reverend Miller, I realized that nobody in this world needs to be so poor they have to sell their bodies to feed their children. So I got good grades and a high SAT score and received a scholarship to Northwestern for my undergraduate degree in economics. I applied to Rhodes because I wanted to show the world that Native American women could become more than whores and waitresses and hotel maids. That we could think and talk for ourselves."

"Now, now," Henry said, getting up and coming over to her chair to pat her long black hair.

She pushed his hand aside. "Stop coddling me, goddammit. I'm not your helpless little sister anymore. I never took a penny of your money to put myself through school, because I wanted to make it on my own. Madelena Spring Rain is my name. I am not a Little Hawk."

"I couldn't be prouder of you, Madelena," Henry responded, kneeling beside her to take her in his arms to stop her trembling. "You are my Spring Rain, and you will always be my little sister. But you are now a grown woman and someone this world must reckon with."

She melted into his arms as Henry stroked her hair. Jenks watched them intently, feeling passions he had so long tried to subdue.

"But back to your arrival and why I asked you to come, Jugs," Henry said, turning to face Jenks. "I've had another vision and I need your help."

Jenks squirmed at the news. Henry had not given him a reason why he'd asked him to come, only said that it was urgent and couldn't be discussed over the phone. "What was the vision, Henry, that brings us back together?"

Jenks remembered Henry's first vision. It had been the summer of their senior year of high school. The two of them, along with Madelena, had driven out to Crazy Horse Monument in the middle of the night. Jenks's dad and mom had gone to the State Fair in Huron and taken his sisters with them. His dad had left him the pickup truck. Driving a stick with just his left arm was a challenge for Jenks, but he'd figured out a way to do it, although he scared the hell out of Henry and Madelena whenever he drove because he had to take his hand off the wheel to shift the truck. Madelena, who usually sat in the middle between Jenks and Henry, had taken up the chore of doing the shifting for him. She had turned it into a game. Jenks would say "ready" when he pushed in the clutch, then she'd shift the gear and respond, "Go." They never did quite get it worked out right and got a lot of gear grinding, but laughed every time, classifying the grinds as small, medium, or large. Occasionally, they'd get a "humongous."

There had been a full moon that night, and the huge white monument in the moonlight seemed to change the color of the sky around it to a deep purple. Henry told Jenks as they gazed at that sky that he was having a vision. It was the first time Jenks had witnessed Henry having one, but he didn't make much of it, knowing that Indians believed in things like that. Seeing Crazy Horse that night against that sky while standing next to Madelena, however, had been something extraordinary for Jenks as well. It was the first time he realized that he was in love with her. He lost his concentration and forgot all about how he had gotten out there or why he'd come. All he was able to think about was her making flower necklaces for him and Henry in the forest when the three of them were out on their adventures. He remembered how much he had wanted to kiss her during those magical days, even though she was four years younger.

"Crazy Horse told me to help our people," Henry had said to Jenks that night. "He said that I could change the world with Madelena and you, but that we had to make a pledge to each other to always stay together, no matter what else might happen to us."

Jenks hadn't been able to take his eyes off the statue, wanting the dream of kissing Madelena to come back to him, but he knew it was never going to be possible. He knew that Henry would kill him if he even looked at Madelena the wrong way, let alone kissed her. Jenks had a massive sweep of vertigo as his mind and body battled with the idea of pledging to always stay together with Henry and Madelena and not ever being able to tell her how he felt.

Henry put his arms around Jenks and Madelena and pulled them into his massive chest. "I pledge my loyalty to both of you forever."

Jenks had felt Henry's raw power and was terrified by it. But even more terrifying was how he felt at the touch of Madelena's soft skin and the smell of her female musk.

Henry had continued, "From this moment on, we are bound in this oath to Crazy Horse to save our people. Say, 'We are one.'"

Jenks heard Madelena say the words. He picked up her love for her brother in her tone and prayed with all his heart that someday, she would use that same tone toward him. Even though he knew it could never be, he wanted nonetheless to ride the magic of that moment and somehow wish it into reality. He repeated Henry's oath back to him and Madelena, desperate enough to take any leap into the unknown to stay together with her and find a way to make his own vision come true.

"Now I will carry our pledge directly to Crazy Horse to prove our resolve and obtain his guardianship forever. I'm going to the top, to the tip of his finger."

Jenks replied, "That's crazy, Henry. That'd take a couple of days, with ropes and pitons, and besides it's illegal and sacrilegious. Not to mention we didn't bring any food or water."

"When I stand on his finger, I'll have all his power. Our pledge will be sacred."

"If you weren't an Indian, people would lock you up in the nut house if they heard you talking like that."

"Don't do it, Henry," Madelena said to her brother, and pressed in closer to Jenks to show she was on his side. It was the first time that she had stood with Jenks against Henry.

"Look at your watch," Henry said to Jenks, shrugging off his sister's plea. "What time is it?"

"I'm not looking at my watch," Jenks responded. "You aren't going, and if we have to, Madelena and I are going to jump on you and hog-tie you."

Henry stared at Jenks with surprise and wrinkled up the skin on his forehead. "Jugs, that's the first time I've ever heard you say something with your balls and not your brain. Damn, I'm proud of you." He gave Jenks a big hug. "You're my best friend," he said. "And now my brother by oath. I will never forget you."

Henry turned and gave Madelena a big hug too. She clung to him, but he unwound her arms from him and wrapped them around Jenks instead. "You take care of her if anything ever happens to me," he said. "You promise?"

"I promise."

"And with that promise, I'll give you mine. I promise I will protect you both, no matter what the evil or the size of the foe."

"Henry, don't go," Jenks had said.

"A warrior needs a cause," Henry replied.

Jenks continued to plead with him. "If I'm your brother now, I can't let you go out and get yourself killed."

"You must learn to understand purpose versus reason," Henry said to him, "and that there are greater powers around us to help us on our journeys. I am going to my greater power now to show my commitment and ask for his help. Have faith in me, my brother, as I will always have in you."

With that, Henry had turned and loped for the monument. He was the lone runner, jumping over rocks and boulders, as light as a deer. Jenks and Madelena lost him in the dark as he disappeared into the heavy boulder debris left over from all the blasting for the monument.

Madelena had begun to shake, her skinny little arms wrapped around Jenks like ropes. She sniffled in the dark. He stroked her hair with his one arm to try to calm her and floated on the scent of her mane that was like pine needles in the warm sun. Passion stirred in his loins as she held onto him, but he quickly shut it off and gently pushed her away. "We must not lose sight of him," he said, to get his mind to take over his body. She nodded and stood next to him, peering into the dark to try to catch a glimpse of Henry, but he was gone.

They waited through the night, never moving from their spot. By daylight, Jenks knew they were going to have to do something. They could get arrested for being where they were, and more, Jenks felt he needed to call the sheriff to get a rescue squad out there from the Forest Service. Jenks imagined Henry lying in a circle of huge rocks, his arms and legs broken.

But then Madelena nudged him and nodded up to the monument. On the outstretched arm of Crazy Horse, something was moving. In comparison to the sculpture, it looked like an insect, but Jenks knew it was Henry. The dissociated

feeling Jenks had felt when they had all taken their oath together came back to him, and the world was no longer the
same place that it had been the day before. He watched as
Henry made his way to the tip of Crazy Horse's outstretched
finger, and although he was too far away to be heard, Jenks
knew that he would be beating his chest in a war cry.

After he and Madelena had lost sight of him again, Jenks
moved the truck off the road so he wouldn't get arrested and
waited anxiously for the whole day. As twilight set in, Jenks
was getting ready to call the sheriff, figuring Henry had killed
himself coming down, but then, just as darkness descended, Henry came dragging toward them, more like a wounded animal than a man. Jenks and Madelena ran for him and
got on either side of him to help him back to the truck. When
they hoisted him into the truck bed, he lay staring up at them,
his lips cracked and bleeding, and his hands, arms, and knees
swirls of mixed wet and dry blood. "Did you see me?" he said,
barely able to talk.

"Yes," they both answered.

"I talked to Crazy Horse. He is happy with our pledge and
will protect us." Henry had then passed out with his head in
Madelena's lap.

Back in the present, Jenks watched Henry face the statue
of his great-great-great grandfather through the huge picture
window. "In my new vision," Henry continued, "Crazy Horse
showed me a land where white people hunted brown people.
This land was covered with thousands of dead brown bodies.
For as far as I could see, piles of putrid and rotting corpses
stretched. Flies covered these bodies like a thick fog, and animals of all shapes and sizes, even other humans, feasted on
them. Grandfather carried me over these ghostly fields for
miles and then across a vast concrete wall patrolled by white
men with guns who shot brown people trying to breach it.

Behind the wall, I saw blooming trees, rich fields of grain, and herds of cattle. White families worked to sow the grain and harvest the fruit. Clusters of homes dotted the landscape, and strange vehicles traveled the roads. The white people all wore glasses with earbuds and microphones through which they communicated to a god who answered their questions and told them what to do."

Jenks shook his head, concerned. "And what is it you are taking away from this vision, Henry?"

"The vote to kill Sentinel in the Senate tomorrow does not look good for us," Henry responded. "I doubt that we will have enough votes to pass the House's bill to stop Kahn's executive order, and Sentinel will go through. If that happens, there are many among the Resistance who will see Sentinel as the portent of a police state and will resist violently. With the degree of hate in our country, that violence could turn into civil war. Race will likely define the sides, regardless of political leaning, and many of my people will be killed. From my vision, I know that I must do everything I can to prevent war from coming."

Jenks studied Henry carefully. "How would you do that?" he asked, glancing over to see what Madelena's reaction was. But she gave away nothing, other than her full attention to her brother.

"If we lose the vote to block Sentinel, we would also likely lose a vote to try to impeach Kahn," Henry replied. "My plan is to begin the referendum process for a constitutional amendment to hold an emergency digital election. We will need control of Sentinel to do that."

Jenks eyed the sandwich Madelena had set down in front of him but had lost the hunger he had arrived with. "And assuming Stanyan immediately implements Sentinel once he's won the vote, how do you plan to take it over?"

Henry smiled broadly. "With you," he said. "I am assuming you can do that."

Jenks glanced quickly at Madelena to see her reaction, but her expression was the same as Henry's.

"You have caught me off guard, Henry," Jenks responded. "Let's just say I could do as you assume. What happens if you don't get the referendum signed for a new election?"

"Then we must ensure Kahn doesn't use Sentinel to enslave us or kill us off," Henry responded.

Jenks rubbed at his forehead. "Taking Sentinel down or taking it over from the government is something that cannot be done without Bur McAnter. He already has a functioning implementation of Sentinel at Eagle's Cliff, and the only way to 'take it over' is to work with him to do it. His Sentinel will be in control of all communications systems—cable, internet, phones, and television—so it would be a very big deal even with McAnter's inside help. McAnter and I would need to be tied at the hip again, like we were for the four years at Cornell when we built Athena, our original creation. But we had a fundamental difference of opinion on how much control we give to her, and so we split. He took the government's offer and built his own version of Athena, which is now Sentinel. But they are very different systems, and I fear Sentinel is open for massive abuse. Athena, on the other hand, is not."

Madelena leaned over to face him. "Athena is not subject to abuse because she would manage us, not the other way around?"

Jenks wrinkled his brow. "You've been reading my work?"

"Yes," she responded. "I've been following you for twenty years. How hard would it be for you to replace McAnter's Sentinel with your original Athena?"

"Fairly easy, technically," Jenks said, "except for the little detail that McAnter and I would have to bring her back up again together. We built her so that both of us must sign on to activate her. Let me just say that when we agreed to kill her, it was a conscious effort on both our parts, so there is a big burned bridge we'd have to rebuild in order to work together. But why would I want to do that?"

"We believe that implementing Athena will help alleviate the hatred that's driving Kahn's followers to start a war," Madelena said.

Jenks tried hard to stay focused, but this is not what he had expected. "Athena is a very scary concept for most people, Madelena, especially right-wingers."

"Not if we fully explain it in terms everyone can understand," Henry said. "Madelena has convinced me that we must move into a new economic and social model."

"I see. Which would require that the people agree to be managed by a machine."

Henry put down his cup on the table and rubbed his hands together. "It is political intervention that is ruining our government today, Jenks, so I believe we are in sync on our objectives as we understand your writings. We want to adopt a totally independent way to run the country and to conduct fair elections. We need to take those operations out of the hands of Man, at least for now."

Jenks rubbed at his forehead again. "I wish it could be that easy, Henry, but Man is going to want to believe he is in control of Athena or Sentinel. Kahn, for example, wants to use Sentinel for his own purposes, and then you may want to use Athena for yours. Either can be very good, or very bad. The reason I split with McAnter is that I'm against either system's adoption without an agreement on how much control we give it and how it's governed."

"You want to give her complete control," Madelena replied. "She makes the decisions and we implement them. We elect leaders who are dedicated to keeping her running, and if we no longer want her in control, we elect leaders to take her down. But we can never change the major canon she was built on: to preserve the greater good."

Henry went on before Jenks could respond. "Madelena's thesis for her PhD at Rhodes is a definition of the greater good, Jugs, and how it could be achieved and maintained by a machine. I think that she can help us explain to the people what Athena could do and what they would be getting into with her."

"If we do indeed lose the vote tomorrow to kill Sentinel," Madelena continued, "we'd like to come back with your Athena as our platform for massive change. We'd use her to conduct a digital election which we know would be impossible to spoof because of the microchip implants she requires for identification."

"A feature that McAnter has duplicated in Sentinel, as you know," Jenks replied. "Which means you'd have to convince all those marching against Sentinel right now because of the implants to reverse their position and say the implants are okay for Athena?"

"If Sentinel passes, we are all going to have to get the implants anyway," Henry said, "so everyone will already have them. Without them, Kahn can shut off our ability to use our phones and computers, so they are going to happen one way or another. With Athena, though, we can use the implants for the very positive purpose of conducting fair elections."

"And us taking over Sentinel happens with or without a war?" Jenks asked.

"Without," Henry answered quickly. "Athena becomes our reason to prevent a war."

"Kahn and the Nationalists don't want to see Athena happen, so they will surely be willing to start the war to stop her. Therefore, you haven't prevented a war from happening; you've just changed who starts it."

"In that case, we use Athena to win the war."

"Those kinds of ideas are going to get you killed."

"We are very well aware of that possibility," Henry said, "but we have to try. We are not going to sit by and let ourselves be wiped out without a fight. With you, we have a chance of making this work without having to go to war. We're asking you to join us, Jugs."

Madelena kneeled beside his chair and took his hand. "I'm asking you to join us."

Jenks did not know how to react. This was all too much for him to take in. And Madelena's touch made it all that much harder. "The trip has caught up to me, I'm afraid," he said, needing to get some time alone. "Is there a blanket or a bed you could spare me? You've given me a great deal to sleep on."

"We have a bedroom ready for you, my old friend," Henry said, coming to his feet. "We can talk more in the morning. Thank you so much for coming. It is truly great to see you again."

CHAPTER 5

BUR MCANTER'S ANGER THREATENED to shut down his self-control as he rushed from the helipad atop DWP headquarters in downtown LA to the utility's underground computer center in the same building. He had no idea what he was about to face, and although he was an expert in cybersecurity, he'd been wracking his brain on the four-hour chopper ride down from Eagle's Cliff, putting together recent threats he'd seen and how he'd dealt with them. On every case he'd dealt with, there was always just a hint of doubt in his mind that this could be the one he couldn't solve.

Among the wall of people waiting for him, he recognized Mayor Padilla and Senator Trujillo. The rest were a mix of uniforms and suits. He shook hands with first the mayor and then the senator. Her gaze was unfriendly, bordering on hostile.

"We are expecting a lot from you, Dr. McAnter," she said, pressing his hand harder than most men he had shaken with. There was an animal-like quality about her so different from his wife. Where Carmen was soft, loving, and nurturing, the senator was hard, cold, and direct. Her SEAL moniker, the Serpent, could not have been more apropos. But Bur also saw in her eyes a glassiness that concerned him, and there was just a slight hesitation in her step that made him feel he needed to steady her. There was a push and a pull about her that left him very unsettled.

"Can someone please brief me on what you know and where you are now?" Bur said to the crowd at large.

A lady with short red hair stepped forward and shook his hand. "I'm Director Endicott from the DWP," she said. "It's an honor to meet you, Dr. McAnter. We have not wiped the servers yet, waiting on your recommendation. We assume you want to try to understand what's inside them." She led him to a workstation and brought up long lists of logs. "Thousands of error messages started around 11:00 a.m., then the system shut down altogether," she said. That was two hours ago now.

Bur sat down in front of the workstation and studied the first pages of error messages. Seeing a familiar pattern, he looked up at the director and the crowd around her. "It looks like you had a virus introduced from an attachment on a trouble ticket," he said, pointing to one of the entries in the logs showing the attempted containment of the virus at first detection.

"We thought our new microvirtualization software could stop any virus," Director Endicott said, pursing her lips.

"Theoretically it should have, but it looks like there were multiple viruses in the attachment, and one of them got through before it was contained and immobilized," Bur replied, relieved that he knew what it was but unsure that he'd be able to convince this audience to let him install Sentinel to kill it and prevent this situation from happening again. Rubbing at his beard, he decided to move toward his plan indirectly and said, "Go ahead and wipe all your servers, and then I will load some software to make sure there are no virus segments left once we reboot the servers. After that, you can restore everything from backup."

"This is Sentinel you're putting on?" the director asked.

"Yes," Bur answered. He didn't have any better shot at convincing them than telling the truth. "And I should inform you that once Sentinel is loaded, it will ultimately control all your systems. I'll show you how to monitor it and manage it, but it will inspect and control all incoming and outgoing traffic once it's installed. It has advanced virus containment services not available on the commercial market."

"And we should just let you do this?" Senator Trujillo drilled him. "Does that not put you and your Sentinel in control over everything we have here, then?"

Bur paused before responding, then said, "Well, if you want to find and kill whatever virus may still be in there, and to prevent any new ones, this is my recommendation."

"That puts us in a bit of a bind, Doctor," the senator went on. "That's why we were scheduled to vote on this invention of yours tomorrow. We really don't want it controlling all our systems or our lives."

"That's up to you," Bur said. "You are going to lose some control in order to gain security. Unfortunately, you can't have it both ways."

"Am I the only one here who feels we're being blackmailed?"

No on in the crowd responded.

Bur took in a deep breath, not having the desire to argue with her. "Senator, Sentinel can do many great things that can help you beyond this specific situation, but none of that can happen unless it can stop the hundreds of thousands of new viruses we see every day. These kinds of attacks are only going to increase. We need the same software on every machine in the country to completely stop them. It is a powerful tool that, in the right hands, can potentially lead us into a whole new age."

"And in the wrong hands?"

"I am not the only person in the world working with this technology, Senator. Obviously, someone else knew and understood the limitations of most containerization systems in the world. But I am pretty certain they have never seen anything like Sentinel. People like you are going to have to decide how and when to use this technology. But it's here. It can't be ignored. It should be harnessed for good. It operates by rules and those rules come from you. I just put them into the system. Right now, with your permission of course, I am going to be loading a bare-bones version of Sentinel. The only rules I am going to give it are to find the virus and kill it and then to prevent additional viruses from getting into your systems. You can put any other rules you want on top of that. But an outage like this won't happen again once I install Sentinel."

"What if it is actually Sentinel in there now with some very malicious rules that someone developed? Perhaps that is why you want to wipe all these servers—so it can't be found."

Bur tried to keep his temper down. "It is important that you trust me, Senator. I am not sure what you are inferring, but implying that I caused something like this with my technology is the deepest wound you could inflict on me." Turning to Director Endicott, he said, "Do you read code? No offense, but I can see you're in management."

Bur's question brought a wave of laughter through the surrounding technical crowd that broke the tension introduced by Senator Trujillo.

"Yes, Doctor, I read and write code," the director said, smiling. "Cal Poly."

"Would you mind explaining this entry in the log file to the senator, since she doesn't seem to believe me? Line by line, if you don't mind."

The director sat down in Bur's chair and started reading code out loud. She went through about ten lines, then the senator interrupted her. "Enough of this. Is it a virus or not?"

"Thousands of simultaneously introduced viruses, Senator, exactly as Dr. McAnter described."

Bur took in a deep breath, feeling he'd won a battle he really didn't want to fight. "Just let me know what you want me to do," he said to the senator, taking his seat back from the director. "I know I can fix your problem. The rest of the intrigue you can bring up with the president and General Stanyan."

Mayor Padilla stepped in. "Let's take this up later, once we get our systems back up," he said.

The senator had more to say, however. "One more question before you begin, Doctor. Is there any way to trace what's in there now back to the perpetrators?"

Bur took his time thinking through what would have to be done. "Possibly. We can try to trace the location of the original self-service trouble ticket that contained the attachment. But there's no guarantee. You have to decide your priorities: getting this cloud back up ASAP or finding out who did it. If we wipe the servers, our only way to trace the attack is through internet records. That could take a while. Our chances of tracing the attack are much higher if we don't wipe the servers, but then we don't get the cloud back up."

The senator knelt directly next to him. "How long will it take to get the cloud back up and trace the internet?" Bur could smell her perspiration, she was so close to him. A primal part of him was aroused, but his mind rapidly overwhelmed that temptation with guilt and fear.

"I can give you a better estimate as soon as I can get to work. I'll need to work with some of my team at the CCC and split the tasks. If all goes well, I'd say we can find out in a couple of hours on the internet records. For the server wipe and installation of Sentinel, about two hours."

"And then how long to get the backups restored?" the senator went on, leaning over with her hands on his desk so her face was inches from his.

Bur turned to face her, seeing the sweat on her brow and smelling cough drops on her breath. "Director Endicott will have to estimate the restore time for her other processes."

The senator rose to face the director, easing the extreme discomfort her presence gave him.

"About four hours for the restore, if all goes well," the director said. "But I actually don't know how the system is going to react to Sentinel, so we should test that before we go live again."

Bur reacted swiftly, relieved to get his mind on something besides the Senator's smell. "No need to test. Sentinel is self-learning. If it discovers any anomalies, it will fix them on the fly. It eliminates the need for laborious testing."

The director nodded, smiling. Turning back to the senator, she said, "I will take Dr. McAnter's word on that. I've never tried anything like this before."

The audience around them milled nervously.

"Just for the sake of argument," the senator continued, bending down next to Bur again, "what if you're wrong and things don't work like you say and we cause some other kind of mess?"

More murmurs and shuffling arose in the crowd.

"I know my system, Senator. I am not wrong, and it will work as I say, out of the box, the first time round." Bur clenched his fingers into his thigh to keep his temper down.

"Director Endicott, what is your opinion of this option?" the senator asked.

"Senator, this is way out of my league," the director answered. "There are only a handful of architects in the world who could fully comprehend what Dr. McAnter is doing, let alone build something that does it. Normally, we would do a proof of concept on something like this in a very contained environment. In this case, we don't have the time."

More grumbling broke out behind them in the crowd.

"Quiet," Aleja said, holding up her hands. She leaned down on one knee next to Bur's workstation again, looking him directly in the eye. "I want you to tell me why you think your plan can work. Is that possibly because you took the system down in the first place?"

"Senator," Chief Santos said loudly, "that is off limits."

She ignored the chief and kept staring at Bur. "Well?"

Bur could feel the raw energy coming off her. She was like a lion ready to pounce, but he was concerned with the glaze in her eyes. "When we presented the implementation plan for Sentinel to Congress earlier this month, we had to have proof that we could install it on any system in a reasonable amount of time. We did many studies to confirm various types of computers and environments. Our benchmark average for very large systems like DWP was two hours."

The senator wiped the sweat from her forehead and responded, "We would be solely in your hands. Ten million people in the LA basin would be in your hands. I am not sure I like those kinds of odds."

Bur knew that if he broke her gaze, he'd lose his entire argument. "I am not working alone. I have two hundred of the world's best computer architects and engineers on my team. This isn't the Bur McAnter show, Senator. This is the CCC."

She stared back at him, narrowing her gaze at him. "You look very tired to me, Doctor.

Give me some confidence you have the energy to get this done for us, even if you do have two hundred helpers."

"I will get this done, Senator. Of that you have my word."

"You didn't answer my first question. Are you confident because you did it in the first place?"

Around them, accusations against Bur from Aleja's Resistance members were countered by objections for her drilling him so hard from Nationalist attendees.

Bur dug his nails into his thigh again. "I did not do this, Senator."

She continued to stare at him. "What if whoever did this is smarter than you?"

He shook his head. "For this application, there is only one person in the world that I know of who smarter than me: Jenks Kennard. He and I built the forerunner of Sentinel together."

"Could this Jenks Kennard have done it, then?"

Bur shook his head, now losing his temper. "Jenks has the highest ethical standards of anyone I've ever known. He would never contemplate using his technology to even hurt a fly."

The senator once again rubbed at her forehead, her eyes wandering around the room. "And for now, we can then conclude that other systems in the city and country are at risk without your Sentinel? That of course has to be your final statement, Doctor?"

"I'm afraid so, Senator. This is a very dangerous world we are living in. Now, what would you like me to do?"

"We must proceed," the mayor came in. "Doctor, should we see any downstream impacts from what you are about to do, we will of course know how to find you."

Bur looked around at the multiple eyes burrowing into him and found another thread of anger to latch onto to get himself through this. "I can assure you I am well aware of the consequences of my actions. With your permission, I'll get to work."

CHAPTER 6

ALEJA HAD TAKEN THREE Tylenols to get rid of her headache, but it was getting worse, as was her fever. She was on her way home to her condo in Venice, driven by LA police. Lights across the LA basin were still out, and she was concerned about the safety of her daughter. She had been unable to get through to Maria because of the phone system overload. The eerie ride through Los Angeles with traffic lights out and stalled cars everywhere made her feel guilty coming home amid the crisis, but she had an overwhelming desire to see her daughter. She had a strange sense that she was dying. She had felt like this on many occasions during her imprisonment in Venezuela. Like then, her mind kept returning to the days of riding horseback in the Malibu hills with her husband and Maria when she had been only nine. That seemed so very long ago now.

Maria ran down the steps of their condo to greet her. "I've been worried sick about you," she said frantically. Then, zeroing in on her mother's sweaty brow and glassy eyes, she gasped. "What happened to you?"

Aleja put her arm around Maria's shoulders and used her as a crutch to get inside. Maria helped her to their living room couch and sat her down. Trying to stop the spinning in her head, Aleja held Maria in her arms and stroked her hair. "Thank God you are all right."

"But you aren't, Momma. Where did you get these clothes?"

"There were smoke bombs filled with anthrax spores in the attack," Aleja explained. "The police washed me down and gave me these fresh clothes. I didn't want to infect you. You don't have to worry now that all the spores have been washed off me. Anthrax is not contagious. I also got a vaccine and antibiotics. I should be better in a couple of days."

"Shouldn't you be in the hospital?" Maria asked nervously, wiping the sweat away from her mother's face with the sleeve of her blouse.

Aleja shook her head. "They are jammed. I am much better being here with you. There's nothing more that can be done anyway. I just have to wait for the vaccine and the antibiotics to kick in."

"You're burning up," Maria said, continuing to dab Aleja's forehead. "We've got to get your temperature down." She put one of her mother's arms around her shoulder and helped her to the bathroom. There, she ran a tub of cool water and helped her in, stripping her down to her underwear first.

The cool water felt good to Aleja and helped clear her head. "I want to give you some instructions, just in case I get any worse," she said to her daughter. "As soon as the phones are working again, please call Senator Little Hawk and have him find out if any of the other Resistance leaders were attacked. I am concerned about the timing of this attack and feel that Kahn was involved. I want you to promise me that no matter how bad you think I am, you will get me back to the DWP tomorrow so that I can hear directly from him what he's found out. I want to be able to look into his eyes."

"Momma..."

"Hush. After that, you must get me to Washington if the Sentinel vote is still on. No matter how sick I am, I must do those two things."

"You need to stay right here and let me get you well," Maria responded, sniffling.

"I should get better, so your mother-henning is unnecessary. But just in case I don't, there isn't going to be anything you can do about it. You must promise me to do these two things. I need you to act like my daughter and kick some ass if you need to, and don't take any shit from anyone. Promise?"

Maria started to cry, wiping Aleja's forehead with a cold washcloth. "I promise..."

Aleja grabbed her daughter's hand and squeezed as hard as she could. "I am counting on you, Maria. You need to be strong—for me. I want to hear you again, but this time with some anger in your voice. Goddammit, I want to catch whoever did this!"

She heard her daughter's defiant shout and smiled. She prayed with all her might that the medicine would work for her and she would not have to put any more of this weight on her daughter's shoulders.

CHAPTER 7

THE LAST PERSON BUR wanted to see right now was President Kahn. He'd been up for twenty-four straight hours since leaving Eagle's Cliff, struggling to get Sentinel uploaded onto the DWP cloud amid the seeming scores of people asking for a status every five minutes. With his fatigue and stress, he kept making simple mistakes, which made it harder to give instructions to the two dozen members from his CCC team who had been brought onsite at the request of the president. Bur had just gotten word that things were finally coming together, and the electricity should be up again within the hour. But just when he was feeling a sense of relief, Kahn walked in.

"Good job, Dr. McAnter!" the president said, striding up to him amid a flock of reporters and secret service agents. "I had no doubt you could fix this malicious attack." He gave Bur a big bear hug.

The president's sudden appearance brought shouts from reporters and protestors: "Are you considering an attack on Iran?"

Bur now could see hundreds more protestors outside on the DWP landing waving their fists and carrying signs, lined up in Resistance versus Nationalist groups on either side of a wall of police. Someone from the Resistance side yelled, "This is what we get for backing out of the Iran nuclear deal!"

On the other side, one of the Nationalists hollered back, "The blood of the LA victims is on your hands, Resistance! We should have had Sentinel months ago!"

Bur watched the latter side boo Senator Trujillo as she arrived with her own entourage. She was being led and steadied by a teenage girl whose eyes were ablaze with anger. The girl brought the senator directly up to Bur, ignoring the president, but making no attempt to shield her comments from him. "My mother wants to talk to you," she said to Bur. "She is very sick and shouldn't be here, but she is. She is risking her life to hear what you have to say."

The senator patted her daughter's arm, then faced Bur directly. Where her eyes had been glassy yesterday, they were almost opaque now, and she had a very deep cough. "Don't worry, anthrax is not contagious," she said.

"A deadly act," Bur responded. "I'm sorry this happened to you."

Her daughter bristled, speaking before her mother could. "Especially if you were the one who started it."

Bur's anger flashed red, but he pulled it back. "I am sorry your mother was attacked," he said. "Hopefully, we can work together now to prevent other people from getting hurt."

The senator pulled her daughter back and said, "Have you fixed the issue and confirmed where the attack came from?"

"I've fixed the issue and do know where the attack came from," Bur answered, turning his attention to the president as he spoke.

"And?" the president said.

Bur shook his head, his anger flashing again. "Iran."

"That confirms the tweet from yesterday, Senator," the president said facing the very sick woman. "I will call for a joint session of Congress tomorrow to discuss our next steps."

"You won't do anything foolish like declaring war before then, will you, Mr. President?" the senator responded between fits of coughing.

"Right now, I am not looking for war," Kahn replied. "I will welcome your input tomorrow, God willing that you are recovered enough by then to come."

"She'll be there," the senator's daughter said, tightening her grip around her mother's waist to keep her standing.

"Indeed, I will," the senator responded. "I am very happy to hear that you are not looking for war, Mr. President. I pray that you will not change your mind."

Kahn shook his head. "I will not change my mind. I very much want the Resistance to be completely on board with whatever next steps we take."

The senator narrowed her eyes in surprise. "I am so encouraged to hear those words from you. While my intuition urges me to be cautious, this certainly sounds like positive news."

"That's all I can hope for," Kahn responded. "I just want to do the right thing to protect our country. I second Dr. McAnter's regret that you have been attacked and want to make sure that nothing like this ever happens again."

Bur watched the president walk away, but the senator stayed behind for a moment, moving in close to him. "Doctor, I may have prematurely judged you. Your concern for not wanting to see any other people get hurt surprised me. If you really do care, I would like to talk to you in more detail—in private. Here is my telephone number." She handed him her card.

Bur took the card and watched her go, surprised and confused. It was hard for him to grasp how her demeanor toward him had changed so substantially since yesterday. He attributed it to her sickness. But Kahn's statement about not wanting to start a war also surprised him. There couldn't be a better time or reason to retaliate against Iran. He'd add these new events to his list of things to contemplate, but for now, his immediate concern was finding out the status of his own family in San Francisco. Even though the cyberattack had been limited to LA, he wasn't sure the anthrax had.

CHAPTER 8

JENKS AWOKE AT THE knock on his bedroom door at 8:00 a.m. Madelena called out to him and invited him to coffee on a private deck, which had a magnificent view of the Crazy Horse Monument. She was wearing workout tights as if she'd just come in from a run.

"We left off last night by asking you to join us in taking over Sentinel. Did you come to an answer?"

The rapid transition from his memories of the past to the present made Jenks very dissociated. "I was thinking about that last night at the blasting shack," he said.

She narrowed her eyes, nodding slowly.

It had been the night of their high school graduation, and there was a big party by the senior class to celebrate both Henry's and Jenks's big successes. Henry had received a football scholarship to Nebraska, after having been sought after by many of the top football schools in the nation. Jenks had won the National Science Fair by developing an antivirus computer plug-in built on AI. The plug-in was so innovative that it landed him national acclaim and a full scholarship to Cornell.

Most of the students that night had been drinking, and Henry and Jenks had joined in for once, even allowing

Madelena to have some shots from the various bottles that were being passed around. By the time the three of them left the party together, they were very drunk. Henry didn't want to go back to his foster home at Reverend Miller's with Madelena drunk, so he made up a story that he and his sister were staying over at Jenks's place. Jenks made up a similar story for his parents that he was staying over at Henry's, and then Henry convinced Jenks and Madelena to go to Crazy Horse and stay overnight in the old abandoned blasting shack at the bottom of the massive carving.

As they were in the process of trying to get an ancient kerosene lamp to work, Henry had to take a pee and had left Jenks and Madelena in the tent to finish getting the lamp lit. When they had finally succeeded, Jenks stood on a rickety old chair and asked her to hand the lamp to him so that he could hang it from the ceiling of the dilapidated shack. In the process, he lost his balance and fell off the chair onto her, knocking her to the floor. He had stared down at her, his face only an inch from hers. He wasn't sure if he'd kissed her first or she'd kissed him, but however it began, neither stopped.

Jenks had been lost in ecstasy when Henry came back in. Jenks would never forget the look in Henry's drunken eyes. "You fucking pervert," Henry had slurred, grabbing Jenks by the back of the neck and pulling him off his sister.

"It was my fault," Madelena cried, stumbling to intervene.

Henry pushed her away, then forced Jenks back against the wall of the shack. "And I called you my friend," he said. "Trusted you with my sister for all these years. You make me sick."

"Henry!" Madelena screamed. "It wasn't his fault. I did it."

"Shut up. I saw what happened. You're just trying to cover up for this deviant."

"Take it back, Henry," she said to him, trembling. "Don't call him that. You can do whatever you want to me, but he did nothing."

"Shut up."

She picked up an ax that had been left behind in the shack and raised it on Henry, staggering to keep her balance she was so drunk. "If you try to hurt him, you'll have to come through me. I'm not afraid of you."

He reached out to take the ax from her, but Jenks intervened, trying to push Henry away from her. Henry growled and shoved Jenks in the chest, sending him flying through the entrance of the shack. There was a brief struggle inside the shack, then Henry came out, carrying Madelena under one arm with her kicking and screaming at him to let her go.

"Never come near me or her again," Henry said to Jenks as he passed him, not looking into his eyes. Jenks had watched them disappear into the night, unable to move.

Coming back to the present, Jenks cringed as he heard her words to Henry that night again in his mind. He could think of nothing he wanted more than to heal what they'd been through in high school.

She reached out and took his hand. "There is much there that we need to come to terms with."

Jenks's stomach churned. "I would like that." He tried to avoid her deep black eyes, but it was impossible for him. "When I envisioned the full implementation of Athena, it was before Kahn came to power. I felt that there would be opposition to it, but the social and economic conditions at the time made it plausible to implement. That's all changed now, and in talking with you and Henry, I understand that many people could die from this idea, including both of you. Please back off this idea of trying to take over Sentinel. Wait until you are back in power through a normal election process in which the people vote in advance for Athena. Right now, this kind of change can't work, and the opposition to it will be large and violent."

She nodded toward the monument. "Remember when Henry made his climb to the top of Crazy Horse?" she said. "We both said he couldn't do it."

"Come on, Madelena, this is far different."

"Is it, Jenks? Henry is leading us; don't forget that. Perhaps for anyone other than Henry, this would be impossible."

Jenks could not help but stare into her eyes. He had his own brief vision of what this would lead to. "I don't want to see you or Henry get hurt, and this is most likely going to get you killed. Please come to your senses. Please listen to my warning."

She got up and faced the monument. Speaking with her back to him, she said, "My grandfather never owned the land or wanted to. He loved it and knew it was for all the people and animals to share. I am of his blood, and I believe my brother's vision. Henry originally wanted to go through the normal election process and run for president, but Kahn's increasingly erratic behavior indicates we are running out of time. I will now give you my warning. If we don't successfully execute this plan to take over Sentinel and call for the people to weigh in immediately on the future direction of our country, Kahn is going to use Sentinel to assist in making Henry's vision of a brown genocide reality. I am begging you to work with us to make our plan happen. Kahn's unquenchable thirst for power will prevent a normal election from ever occurring."

Jenks looked at Madelena against the carving of her great-great-great-grandfather above them and knew she shared the same heritage as Henry. There was a part of them he would never know or understand, which both intrigued and terrified him. Madelena's warning rang in his ears, and he felt a powerful energy coming off the mountain. And then suddenly, Henry appeared.

"I can see you two are in a big argument," Henry said, smiling. "Just kidding. Mind if I join? I'd love to hear your vision of Athena, Sentinel's predecessor."

Jenks shook his head to clear it, totally unbalanced by the synchronicity of Henry's arrival with the conversation he was just having with Madelena. He paused to collect himself, feeling Henry had a much deeper intent with his question than met the ear, and that his answer must somehow justify his life for the past twenty years. Choosing his words carefully, he began slowly. "Think of Athena as an all-seeing cloud of awareness that can capture information and turn it into knowledge. That awareness is built upon machine learning, artificial intelligence, and the concept of intent-based processing.

"She can spawn and manage thousands or even millions of service agents to gather data from virtually any source that she can access digitally, visually, or by sound, and then she determines the intent of the action or actions that created the data through AI algorithms. She connects the intent with the context of the situation and solves the problem or answers the question. She then *knows* how and why the action occurred and adds that knowledge to her ever-growing cloud of awareness. As her cloud grows, she becomes totally self-managing, without the need for any human intervention. She will know what to do in any situation. Whatever action she takes or question she answers will always be correct, because of the extensive predictive analysis she performs before she responds. She weighs each alternative and predicts what would happen in each case, then selects the one that meets her basic canon: to preserve the greater good. Over time, these analyses become truth through machine learning. As her base of truth grows, her decisions come faster and faster."

"So Athena can then think?" Henry asked.

"Yes, in a way of speaking, if you call thinking the intent to understand. She operates totally under the objective of knowing not only how something happened but why. With this breadth of knowledge, she is not only able to answer any question, but she can manage any process, company, city, state, or country. She operates only by logic. She has no ego, fears, or delusions to influence her. She works much like the human brain via neural networks, but she never forgets anything. Just think of how powerful any of the three of us could be if we could remember everything we've seen or experienced within nanoseconds and apply it to the situation in which we find ourselves. Athena can *know* everything theoretically, given enough storage and processing power to operate her infinite memory. Modern technology now provides us that power."

"So she is indeed like a god, then," Madelena said.

"Yes, she is," Jenks replied. "Some might argue she is more powerful than a god, though, because she can actually carry on a real-time conversation with us, and we can witness her power directly. She can truly rule the world, if we let her."

"And do you think we should?" Henry asked.

Jenks paused for another long moment. "I have very little faith in mankind, Henry. Fortunately, our great gifts of self-awareness and conscience allow us to understand that we need something outside ourselves that is impervious to our weaknesses and can thus do a better job of managing us than we can. We are on the verge of annihilating not only our own species but the world around us."

Madelena asked, "How long would it take to get Athena in control of everything?"

Jenks pursed his lips and shook his head. "If the vote for Sentinel passes, McAnter will load Sentinel on every computer and device in the country. I'm sure he has worked it out so that it won't take much longer than downloading the latest version of the operating system on your iPhone. And once it is loaded, it starts gathering information about each location and each person's actions, and then sending that information back to its cloud of awareness. That surveillance information is precisely why Kahn sees Sentinel as the perfect vehicle for not only preventing terrorist attacks, but also knowing what his enemies are up to. Knowledge is power and he will have almost unlimited access to anything he wants to know."

"And he will indeed use it," Henry replied. "With Sentinel, he could become nearly invincible."

Jenks shook his head. "Sentinel does not have Athena's power to become self-managing. Sentinel lacks the predictive analysis algorithms that allow Athena to always know what to do based upon the truth. She continues to learn, applying her advanced AI to establish truth as it relates to her basic canon of fostering the greater good. And with this truth, she can define right and wrong, and can reward and punish."

"Which is what Kahn will want to do all by himself," Madelena said.

Jenks nodded. "There is a point in history where Man must make the decision to let her manage him, for the sake of his own survival. This kind of decision will only be made by necessity, in a time when there is no other choice, after all else has failed. What we must decide is if we are at that point. We either make the one-time decision to let Athena manage us or not, and if we do, there is no turning back."

Jenks began pacing, remembering the day he and Bur McAnter had parted. Bur had come into Jenks's office at Cornell and sat down across from him as he had done a thousand times before in the past four years while they had developed Athena.

"I've decided to take the government's offer," McAnter had said to Jenks. "I really believe Kahn can make our dream a reality."

"Even though you've never discussed the small detail of Athena's Total Control with him or the air force?"

"I will in time, Jenks. We've got to take it a step at a time. I really want you to come with me."

Jenks shook his head slowly. "We've had this discussion many times, Bur. I won't come and I won't agree to give you the source code. So you will have to build Athena all over again from scratch."

"I'm prepared to do that, Jenks, but it's going to be without Total Control for now. In time yes, but Total Control is just too much for anyone to swallow at this time."

"What about the master canon for the greater good?"

"The master canon will be there. But Sentinel will be controlled by the president and Congress."

Jenks had known it would do no good to argue with him any longer. "What happens to the existing master?"

"You can keep it, Jenks. There's not much you'll be able to do with it, though; I am not going to allow you to modify the dead man's switch to allow only you to bring it up every day. It will still take both of us. So the system will remain ours together, should we ever decide to reunite, which I truly hope we do. But for now, Athena is dead."

Jenks came out of the past and relayed his last meeting with Bur to Henry and Madelena.

Henry responded first. "So where does that put us now?"

"If you lose the vote tomorrow, I will do what I can to get McAnter to work with us to take control of Sentinel and replace it with Athena. But only if we all agree to the concept of Total Control. Otherwise, Athena will remain dead forever."

"We agree," Henry said, looking to Madelena for confirmation. She nodded and took Jenks's hand in hers. "It's the right and only decision, Jenks. There is no other choice but war, and we must take drastic measures to prevent that."

Jenks stared into her black eyes, fearing what lay ahead for them. Even if he could never be together with her romantically, he wanted no harm to come to her.

CHAPTER 9

THE DAY AFTER MEETING with the president at the DWP in LA, Aleja arrived in Washington. She fought off her dizziness and fatigue from her long trip as she entered the House Chamber for the joint session the president had called. She had slept the entire flight from LA, but it hadn't helped. Her cough was getting worse, and at times she felt it was not going to stop. Maria had kept her promise about bringing her here, despite the protestations of her district staff. As she arrived at the front steps of Congress, Henry Little Hawk met her and virtually carried her into the chambers with one of his massive arms around her waist. At her entrance, the Congress buzzed with energy. Members of the Resistance rushed to offer her their well wishes. Even her enemies from the other side of the aisle came to welcome her. She took her seat with Maria on one side and Senator Little Hawk on the other.

The Speaker of the House gaveled the room to silence as the president entered, flanked by the secretary of defense and the joint chiefs.

She tried to contain her anger as Kahn strutted up to the stage to the raucous applause of the Nationalists. She wanted to stand up and boo with an equal show of force from her own party, but restrained herself, knowing this was not the time to start the fight, and not for her to do it. Best for Henry to take the fight today if necessary, since she was not up to it. The main question on her mind was whether Kahn would change his mind about war.

Kahn began. "Members of Congress, we face a historic decision here today, perhaps for the very survival of our country. The vicious attack in Los Angeles two days ago may only be the first of what we will see in the future. It is time we prepare for whatever may come our way."

The Nationalists came to their feet in applause. The Resistance remained seated.

The president went on when the applause died down. "We are now certain the attack came from Iran, despite their protestations of innocence, and we must decide how to respond. As I see it, we have two choices. We can counterattack, or we can succumb to their blackmail and become the laughingstock of the earth. My preference is to send them a clear message."

The Nationalists greeted this with deafening applause, making Aleja's already massive headache even worse. She turned to urge her followers not to respond. She wanted to hear what else Kahn had to say.

"But I want to be clear on what our message is, and I do not want to declare war on them," Kahn stated. "I repeat, I do not want to declare war. What I want is a regime change, to put power in the hands of someone who can lead Iran into this century. Therefore, today, I am asking for your approval to execute a tactical strike against Iran's key military locations, to let them know we cannot be attacked. There will be no civilian targets and conventional weapons only. No nukes. I repeat, no nukes! With this operation, I want to send a message that rather than lifting sanctions, we will now double them, unless they carry out a regime change on their own. And should they make any further attacks on our country, I will use nukes to take out Tehran. They can do their own math on how many thousands of people they would lose as the result of a second infraction against us."

The Nationalists applauded again.

Facing Aleja, he said, "Senator Trujillo, I told you yesterday that I was not looking to go to war, and I hope you see that I have not reversed my position. I would like to ask for your support and the support of your Resistance for this initiative. We have to show a strong, consolidated front to the rest of the world to prevent further attacks. That means the House must approve funding for this initiative."

Aleja was surprised by Kahn's proposal. Encouraged, she rose to her feet to ask some questions. But as she tried to talk, a coughing spasm forced her to sit back down. She motioned for Senator Little Hawk to take over.

The bull of a man came to his feet, creating a nervous rustle in the Resistance behind him. "Are there any other actions you have in mind in addition to this pinpoint conventional attack?" he said to the president.

"There are two segments of my plan, Senator Little Hawk. First, we need to proceed immediately with the rollout of Sentinel across the nation. This will give us protection from further cyberattacks and will allow us to identify everyone in the country so that foreign agents cannot gallivant through our streets at will slaughtering our good people. I am recommending a shortened version of Sentinel, Phase 1 only, which would install Sentinel on every system in the country so that they cannot be penetrated again. We would also need the chip implants so that we can identify and protect each and every citizen of our country and know for certain who is not a citizen. That is as far as we will take Sentinel for now, and then as we get more experience and hopefully buy-in from you, the Resistance, we can discuss Phase 2, the digital economy."

Whispering and sidebars broke out on both sides of the aisle.

Kahn went on. "Second, I am proposing to create and distribute enough anthrax vaccine for the entire country. I have asked Director Shaw of the CDC to join us today to discuss what we know about the anthrax attack in Los Angeles and what we can do about it."

A tall, slender, middle-aged woman with shoulder-length gray hair took the stage with the president. She wore a gray uniform with the red CDC insignia on either arm. "We have concluded from studying the anthrax spores from the canister attacks that this is a new strain of anthrax," she began. "It is not clear yet if our existing vaccine will be effective in stopping the spread of the bacteria in those who have inhaled the spores. For now, at least, the first of three required doses of antibiotics along with the vaccine may be masking the impact of the bacteria, making people feel temporarily better."

The chamber erupted with grumbling on both sides of the aisle. Maria screamed and threw her arms around her mother. Many of the Resistance reached over to touch Aleja. She took the news with shock but not surprise. She knew she was getting worse.

The director went on. "We have for some time been looking for a single-dose vaccine that could be applied in a highly repeatable and rapidly distributable aseptic model—that is, needing no refrigeration. We have been watching a German company called Biosafe that has developed a single-dose vaccine delivered through a nasal spray and not requiring refrigeration or antibiotics. From the tests we have seen on this vaccine, it appears to be far more advanced than what we currently have. When we brought this information to President

Kahn, he asked if Biosafe had three hundred and fifty million doses of this vaccine, and the answer was no. They currently have only about twenty thousand. To produce three hundred and fifty million doses in a short period of time, Biosafe would have to vastly increase their production lines, which could take at least six weeks. But the cost of this would be in the hundreds of millions of dollars and would have to be passed along in the cost of the vaccines. That cost would be prohibitive for most Americans, unless we, the United States government, subsidized this operation."

Grumbling once again broke out in the chamber.

President Kahn came back in to quiet them. "While the cost is very high, I believe it is worth every penny to protect our entire population," he said. "We have considered a phased approach, where we take what vaccine we can get and apply that amount reactively to any areas attacked, specifically now in Los Angeles. We build up the supply over time, as Biosafe produces more vaccine with their current production capabilities. These early supplies would go to our schools, hospitals, military, and police. Then, as we are able to vastly increase production, we distribute the vaccine in a big bang approach so that there is no accusation of political prioritization of who gets the vaccine first. And we will make the inoculation mandatory and free.

"We believe that through the microchip implants that are part of Sentinel, we can be sure that all of our citizens receive their dose. Sentinel will allow us to much more efficiently track who has received their vaccines and who hasn't. We will work initially on just the anthrax vaccines, but in order to assure the safety of our people going forward, we must create other vaccines as well that can shield us from other types of bioterrorist attacks. I am asking for your approval today to fund this anthrax vaccination program and to expand the CDC to investigate similar programs for other biothreats. The estimated cost of this program is ten billion dollars. Sentinel has already been funded through our cyber defense budget, including the almost three hundred million microchip implant kits, so there is no additional cost for that. Regarding timeline, I believe both initiatives must begin at the same time. Our estimates are about six weeks for both to be ready for rollout, including the microchip implants. We must move at once in order to be ready for subsequent attacks."

Both sides of the chamber erupted, but Kahn held up his hands for silence. "I will take your questions now."

Henry Little Hawk came to his feet, facing the other members of Congress before focusing his attention on the president. "Regarding the chip implants, what will you do for those not willing to insert them?"

"Excellent question, Senator. We must work together to convince our people that everyone should have the microchips, for both their own personal safety and the safety of the nation."

More chatter broke out across the chamber. Kahn was in the process of quieting them again when he was interrupted by Director Shaw from the CDC, who had just been approached by an aide with a message. Kahn talked with the director for several moments privately and then beckoned her to step back in front of the microphone.

"I have just been informed that we have seen a number of new deaths in the last six hours, even among those who have had the vaccine," she said. "We have contacted Biosafe and they are in process of sending us twenty thousand doses of their vaccine, which is their current supply, considering they are still in the testing phase. This will cover all those who have been infected, in addition to a reserve for any new threats, but we will not have it for at least forty-eight hours.

Until then, it is difficult to tell how much the antibiotics alone can combat the spores' toxins."

The president took over the microphone once again and turned to Aleja, saying, "I pray that you will be able to survive until then with the antibiotics alone, but many may not. People will be even more terrified with this news. They will want to see us do everything single thing in our power to prevent further attacks. I could use your help in convincing others in your party, both here and across the nation, to cooperate for the good of the country. To ensure you will survive this attack, I will personally bring one of the doses from Biosafe directly to you."

The Resistance became silent.

Facing the entire Resistance now, he said, "With your vote today, we move forward together. May I have your vote?"

Aleja realized that she and the Resistance had no choice but to agree. She turned to Henry, and then to the Resistance, and nodded.

Little Hawk came to his feet in front of his followers. "Any nays?"

The Resistance remained silent.

Little Hawk turned back to the president. "You have our support, Mr. President. For the good of the country."

CHAPTER 10

MARIA HAD BROUGHT HER mother home to their Venice condo after the joint session in Washington three days before. Even though her mother should be in a hospital, she had refused to go, in order to give her spot to other anthrax victims in worse condition than she. Maria had therefore hired a private nurse to be with her twenty-four hours a day. The nurse had put her on oxygen and a morphine drip to help allay her cough. Maria was dabbing her from head to foot with cold ice packs to keep her temperature down when her mother's administrative aide came into the room.

"Sorry to bother you, but we have visitors," the aide said.

Maria looked up and shook her head. "Tell them we aren't seeing anyone."

"It's President Kahn and Director Shaw from the CDC. And a couple dozen reporters. They've brought the new vaccine."

Maria dropped her ice pack and rushed for the front room. The president stepped in to meet her and gave her a big hug. "Everything is going to be okay," he said to her, making sure the camera crews behind him had a good angle on them. "We're going to take care of your mom and get her well."

Director Shaw came in and also gave her a hug. She was wearing a white lab coat and had a nasal spray container in her hand. "I will personally deliver the vaccine," she said to Maria. "That okay? I am a doctor."

"Of course!" Maria exclaimed. "Come on! She's dying."

Maria led the director to her mother's room, followed by the president and as many reporters as could fit into the small condo. Director Shaw removed Aleja's oxygen mask, applied the nasal spray, and then replaced the mask.

The click of cameras annoyed Maria, as did Kahn's talk about how the spray would soon be delivered to hospitals and clinics all over the LA basin. "How long will it take to know if it worked?" Maria asked Director Shaw.

"We should know in twenty-four hours," Shaw answered. Turning to the nurse, she said, "Keep her on oxygen and increase her saline."

Kahn stepped closer to Aleja now, bending over her. "I don't know if you can understand what I'm saying, but I want you to know I'm praying for you. I will be monitoring your status on an hourly basis. I know that I am speaking for the whole country when I say we are all praying for you to get well. We have hurt Iran badly for what they did to you and to thousands of our fellow citizens, but we can't let our guard down."

Turning back to the cameras, he said, "We soon will be installing Sentinel on our internet infrastructure, which will protect every computer and phone in the county from hacking. At the same time, we are creating the CNID, the Consolidated National Intelligence Database, which will hold master identification information for every citizen in our country so that no one's identity can ever be stolen again. Once the CNID is created, we will use it to send out the self-service microchip implant kits that will allow our public safety and medical communities to know the whereabouts, health, and safety of every citizen in our country. These chips are harmless and just go slightly under the skin of the hand. Think of these chips as your key to total safety, no matter where you are, any time of day. I should also explain that with this technology, we can now determine who does not have a chip, and that is the primary purpose of this exercise. For certain, you won't get a chip if you aren't in the CNID. And if someone tries to steal it from you once it's been activated, it won't work, because it memorizes your ECG heart rate signature, the newest form of bioauthentication. I want to also add that if someone tried to steal one of these chips, it would do them no good, because the final verification is your age, sex, blood type, and facial recognition, which we will gather from your driver's license, passport, or other forms of ID. Those without any type of current ID card must obtain one immediately. Your microchip will not be sent until your photo and other identification information is in the CNID. We've tried to make this as painless as possible for everyone and hope you understand that these steps are absolutely critical to your personal safety and the safety of our nation."

Maria was not happy with the barrage of questions from reporters that came after Kahn's statement. She continued her cold pack treatment not only to sooth her mother, but to keep her own mind off what Kahn was saying. When he and the others finally left, Maria knew there was nothing more she could do now but wait and pray. She laid her head down on her mother's bed and fell asleep.

CHAPTER 11

BUR HAD BEEN FLOWN back by helicopter to the CCC at Eagle's Cliff directly after he had installed Sentinel at the DWP and ensured his installation worked. It had now been three days since he'd talked to his family, and he hurried to his office to call them. Even though he'd texted them several times and they had seen him on TV at the DWP, he desperately wanted to hear their voices to be sure they really were okay. Stanyan interrupted him before he could make the call, however. He closed the door of the office behind him so they could be alone.

"Congratulations!" he said, extending his hand. "Your work was a great success. You've got the confidence of most of the nation, at least. But after the strike yesterday on Iran, we feel we must move much more rapidly than we had originally planned and get Sentinel installed on all the networks and servers across the country. I know you are tired, but I'd like to start the download process immediately. I've had Vanderhurst contact the appropriate providers and they're all waiting for your direction."

Bur took a deep breath. "Okay, no problem."

"We'll release the Sentinel installation packs on the download sites. We're counting on your setup routines to be flawless. We're assuming there will be a lot of questions from the installers. You and your team are going to need to be troubleshooting round the clock. Taking over complete control of the web is not going to be easy. We can't be sure, but there may be pockets of the Resistance who are very much against this, so we have to watch carefully."

"Of course," Bur responded. "Are we also turning on the surveillance satellites now?"

"Yes, we want them to be active when the microchips are distributed. It will be nice for us to have eyes in space connected to Sentinel to identify people without the implants. Combined with our eyes on the street—our law enforcement people with handheld scanners—we'll be able to track who and how many people aren't implanting the chips after they're distributed. The first shipments should be going out by end of week, assuming we have the CNID built by then."

"Say what?" Bur exclaimed. "I'm not a magician. There's no way we can get the whole CNID built by end of week."

Stanyan nodded. "You and I know that, but Kahn has no comprehension of technology. For the microchip implant distribution, we'll have to settle for records of what devices are in each household. We can get most of what we need from the device manufacturers as well as the cable companies. For the vaccines, though, we need to know everything we can about every person who gets a dose. That's why we have to encourage people to get their IDs if they don't already have them so we can enter them into the CNID. With your recent fame at the DWP, you're now the face of Sentinel, and you're going to need to help us sell the registration process to the immigrants in our country. It is essential we know exactly who has not been vaccinated."

"That's going to be a tough sell," Bur said, knowing the distrust of Kahn in the Latino community.

"The president is going to be making an announcement soon, discontinuing all ICE activities and also allowing the vaccines for any asylum seekers if they agree to register and get a chip implant. There is a limited amount of vaccine, and we have to make sure we provide it to people who are willing to live by our laws."

The statement surprised Bur, who hadn't heard any of this before. He knew just how hard it would be. His wife, Carmen, was Latina. Even though she and her family were all American citizens, they had brought over extended family who were not. He was trying to picture how his wife and her family would react to him making this request over TV. "I need to talk to my wife," he said.

"Sorry," Stanyan replied, "that's going to have to wait a little longer. You need to get the Sentinel download going ASAP. Don't worry; your wife will forgive you. You're going to be a national hero."

Bur followed orders and assembled his full team to give the command to activate the download sites. The most demanding and immediate problem was to get Sentinel loaded onto the Metropolitan Area Exchanges and Network Access Points that controlled all internet traffic. Regional and local internet service providers would then be forced to load Sentinel to access the MAEs and NAPs. While Bur and his team had done many simulations of this download process, the internet would be down for eight to twelve hours—if all went well. If they had to abort for any reason, the clock started all over again.

Bur took command of the control center and joined the videoconference that had been set up by Vanderhurst with the directors of the three MAEs and five NAPs. Bur was surprised to see government agents standing in the background of each of the locations. While he had always suspected the risk of sabotage or subversion, he hadn't expected these many goons in suits at computer centers. He sat next to Vanderhurst, the second-in-command, who, like him, was a direct report to Stanyan. Bur had never liked that arrangement, but there was nothing he could do about it. Vanderhurst had individual conferencing sessions in progress between their CCC team members and the technical counterparts on the target sites. All activity on the sites was being monitored by a large dashboard on the wall of the Control Center.

Bur scanned the green lights on the dashboard and signaled for the download kits to be released. As he watched the early progress of the downloads, he began to see a slowdown on one of the MAEs. He got up and went to the member of his team working with that MAE technician.

"Looks like another upload is running at the same time as ours," his own engineer said.

Bur took a closer look at the screen. "What are you running?" he asked the MAE technician.

"Nothing. What are you talking about?"

Bur motioned his engineer to get up so he could take over. Then to the MAE technician, he said, "Give me control of your system."

"Why? I know what I'm doing."

"Either you give me control or we find someone who will."

Stanyan picked up on the exchange. He came over to Bur. "What's going on?"

"Another upload is happening on the West MAE. I need to see what it is."

Stanyan addressed the director of the West MAE over Bur's shoulder. "We need access to that workstation now."

The director disappeared from Bur's monitor and reappeared, flanked by federal officers who ordered the technician to get up.

The technician refused to leave his workstation. The officers quickly yanked him away.

"Abort!" Bur hollered across the command center.

"What the hell are you doing?" Stanyan demanded.

"Something just killed the Sentinel upload," Bur replied, "but we're still seeing activity in that set of servers. Something else is being uploaded."

"How the hell can that happen?" Stanyan said. "I thought Sentinel was software on steroids."

"It looks like a virus was teed off at the same time as our download. All these MAEs need to come down now before the virus spreads down to the regional ESPs. Whoever did this is no amateur."

The MAE director suddenly shouted, "Long live the Resistance! We will shut down the internet indefinitely if any further attempts to install Sentinel proceed."

Bur stared at the powerful director, one of the true geniuses of the modern internet, and knew he very well could do what he'd just threatened, especially with the pack of internet specialists behind him. The high-tech community was one of the leading voices of the Resistance.

Stanyan leaned down in front of Bur's videoconferencing camera, staring intently at the director across the virtual bridge. "Director, and everyone else on this call who is part of the Resistance, focus your attention on this feed." Stanyan pulled out his handheld and brought up a video stream of a beautiful redheaded woman and three teenage children. "We have similar streams on the families and loved ones of everyone on this call. You can imagine the perils your families face from our many foes, including the spies and assassins from

Iran, not to mention radical nationalists on our own soil. I can assure you that danger is imminent for anyone not under our protection."

"Bullshit!" the director shouted. "You can't do that. We'll feed this interchange across the country in five minutes if you make any kind of move on my family or anyone else's."

Several other directors chimed in with similar shouts and promises, as did most of the computer techs from the MAEs and NAPs that Bur's team was working with. But as the threats from the Resistance poured through the videoconference bridges, Bur could see goons flooding into the background with weapons drawn.

"You must think we are totally naive not to have expected this," Stanyan called back over the videoconference. "This exchange is going nowhere, and neither are any of you. You will do as I say, or we will methodically start arresting your families until you are ready to pledge your loyalty to the president."

The director eyed the weapons pointed at him, then looked into the monitor to see that other men with guns had invaded his home and surrounded his wife and family.

"We arrest and handcuff your family in order of their age," Stanyan said to the director. "First goes your youngest, Rebecca. Twelve, isn't she? Soccer player, budding thespian?"

The armed men on the video grabbed the girl and held her, forcing her arms behind her back to be cuffed.

"I am going to count to five," Stanyan said to the director. "You give me your pledge, or we go to your sons and your wife. Where we take them is going to be crawling with rapists and gang members. One, two, three, four..."

"Stop!" the director cried.

"Give me your pledge."

The director stared at Stanyan over his monitor. "You have my pledge," he said through gritted teeth.

The armed men released the terrified girl and moved away from the rest of the director's family.

"Now the rest of you," Stanyan said. "Each of my teams at your sites has the jurisdiction to start their own countdowns and do what they need to do to get your attention."

Bur watched in horror as the others in the multiple video-conferences around the room gave their pledges. As much as he hated the Resistance, these techies were his community, and he didn't like to see them threatened.

"Now," Stanyan said when all the pledges had come in from his various field teams, "I want to make it clear that there will be no benefit of the doubt for any mistakes or omissions you might make as we continue this exercise. The next fuck-up we see, someone is going to go to our new holding camps for insurgents. I can assure you there will be some ba-dasses in those camps who are not going to like rich people. If we can't determine where the fuck-up came from, then we are going to randomly select one of your families for arrest. No matter how clever you are to avoid detection, it doesn't matter. One of your friends' or coworkers' families is going to go behind our razor-wire fences in our outdoor retention centers. There will be no beds, blankets, or toilets there, and not the best food or water, assuming the roaming gangs don't steal them from you first. We don't want to see that happen, but we will do what we have to in order to ensure we protect our country."

Stanyan nodded to Bur to begin the Sentinel installation again. Bur took in a deep breath and followed the order. Whatever anger he had felt over the past few days against the Resistance had suddenly changed as it occurred to him that his own family might be at risk if for any reason he refused orders. He wrestled the thought away, knowing he was far too tired to think rationally now.

CHAPTER 12

PRESIDENT RONALD KAHN LOOKED out the window of the Army One chopper, down onto the barbed-wire boundaries of the newly completed Virginia Detention Center twenty miles outside Washington DC. With him was General Herman "Herm" Lancaster, his army chief of staff. The chopper banked and sat down in the middle of the camp. When they got out, the general walked him around the camp.

"These are the latrines," the general said, pointing to a dozen cement canals, each about one hundred meters in length and four meters wide. "You piss and shit into these." He led the president over to the edge of one of the canals. "You have to squat to shit, unless you're a woman; then you have to squat to pee and shit. Once a month, we throw in a couple of tons of lye to decompose the waste. Much cheaper and more efficient than toilets."

"Mind if I use it?" Kahn said, unzipping his pants. Only a few secret service men and soldiers were around. "Long ride down here. Can't make it back to Washington unless we stop at a rest stop."

Herm laughed and joined the president. Both men had no trouble shooting their streams to the other side of the canal.

"We don't want anyone to like being here," Herm said as they zipped up. "It's going to stink all the time. No designation of male or female latrines. You got to go, you use whatever opening you can find."

He walked the president over to a hundred rows of green military tents about six feet high and twenty feet wide. "We plan to get twenty detainees in each tent." He pulled back the canvas lap and stepped in. Rows of military blankets were stacked against the walls. "No furniture. You sleep right on the ground and wrap your blanket around you. Each tent will have to determine their pecking order," he said, smiling. "We will segregate these by sex and families."

He continued on to another row of larger tents, these about twenty-five meters long and fifteen meters wide. Inside was a single row of tables, but no chairs. "We set the food and water out on the tables. Each tent has enough food and water per day to sustain two thousand people. We have twenty of these tents."

Walking back outside, the general led Kahn to the perimeter of the camp, where there was a steel entrance gate. "Once a day, we bring in food and water trucks. Soldiers empty the food into the tents and the water into that little reservoir over there. There are no guards within the camps. They are left to whatever laws take shape on their own. Only rule here is that if you attack a soldier or try to rush the trucks, you get shot."

He continued to walk to a large concrete pit, fifty meters in diameter and twenty meters deep. "This is the burial pit. Anyone who dies or gets shot, ends up here. We don't plan to go through the camp to pick up any bodies. If the detainees want to get rid of the bodies, they bring them here. We wait till either the pit is getting pretty full or pretty smelly before we fire it with napalm."

"Jesus. That is awful," Kahn said, shaking his head.

"Absolutely," the general said, narrowing his eyes as he looked out over the camp. "We want people to want to get the hell out of here. We figure most will break within forty-eight hours and agree to take the pledge and get the butt implants. No hand chips in here. We have high-powered air guns that shoot the chips into their asses. No way to get them out without probably bleeding to death. And these chips are special. They have a teeny cyanide dot on an RFI chip inside. We can send a special signal to the chip to explode the dot. Nobody coming out of here is ever going to break the law again. We make sure to make sure everyone knows exactly how this works. There are no second chances in here."

"Gives me the creeps," Kahn said.

Herm rubbed at his own butt sarcastically. "We are going to need body handlers and gravediggers by the thousands. You can go ahead and let all the Mexicans in who want to come, and they'll come right here. And then we'll have them do whatever we want them to."

"Let's go over the overall setup," Kahn said, heading back for the chopper.

Herm made sure the president had a Diet Coke before he gave the order to lift off. As they circled over the camp again, he said, "We're building two hundred of these across the country. This is one of the largest. The others will be built to accommodate the population density of the area. We are estimating an initial detention of about two million, composed of Resistance militants, illegal immigrants, Iranians living in America, gangbangers, and generally anyone who doesn't have a chip implant. We believe that word from these camps will get out rapidly to motivate those who are able to get an implant to get it done—pronto. If our projections are right, the camps will turn over within forty-eight hours. So we have a steady stream in and a steady stream out."

"What happens if people don't leave?"

"Well, the camps fill up then. Food and water are likely to be short—you get the picture. That should increase the velocity of chip adoption and camp exit."

Kahn took his eyes away from the site below and sipped at his Diet Coke. "What do you need to staff these?"

"We need to get the draft going ASAP," Herm responded. "Five processes: protection, roundup, transport, sustenance, and cleanup. Let me go into detail for each. First, we know the Resistance is well armed and ready to fight, given the slightest provocation. We need to hit them hard and lightning fast if they do. Think of it as a blitzkrieg." He laughed. "Once that initial battle with the Resistance is won, we can move to round up the illegals, Iranians, and bangers. There will be two types of roundups: dead and living. The key is to get a perimeter established around the targets so we can contain damage to public and private property, especially infrastructure. We've plotted out the areas where we expect the largest number of targets. We'll focus our troops there. We're looking to draft about two hundred thousand total soldiers that will all be on protection and roundup initially, then branch off to the other processes. Around the perimeters of the targets, we would have lines of buses. Once we close the perimeter, we round the protestors into the buses. Those that resist and get killed or injured, we leave lying till we get the living out and on their way to the camps. Once the buses have left, we bring in the dump trucks for the dead and injured. Buses and trucks both go to the camps. Dead and injured go into the fire pits while those from the buses are busy trying to get into a safe tent— you get the picture. They figure out pretty fast resistance is not a good idea."

Kahn cringed. "None of this gets out. I will handle the press if they start snooping around. But come to think of it,

I kind of hope they do. It would seem to me you'd only have a few days of this scale of roundup. What happens after that?"

"Well, people aren't going to go to protests anymore. They are going to start acting in small groups or individually. Those teams who had been working the initial roundups would then go to street patrol, potentially building by building or house by house, seeking lawbreakers."

"You've got to be careful not to stop commerce and prevent people from going to work," Kahn said. "After the first roundups, you need to be much lower-key."

"Yes, sir, will do."

"For the two hundred thousand draftees, where do we put them, and how do we train them?" Kahn continued.

"This is going to have to be a citizen army," the general answered. "Housed and fed where they now live. They will report into area operations centers every day. We'll go with simple identification: red caps. We'll put our arms and munitions supplies near the operation centers to equip them. Considering direct staffing for the four elements and indirect staffing to equip and maintain them, we'll put all unemployed law-abiding citizens to work. The rest will go into the camps until they become law-abiding." He snickered.

Kahn looked down at the beautiful hills of Virginia as they headed back for the capital. "The scale of this thing still bothers me," he said. "On paper, it sounds good, but I am very concerned about the operational aspects."

"A population in fear, Mr. President, is relatively easy to control once the leaders are silenced and the fear is instilled permanently among any dissenters. Have faith; this is going to work. We have a very impressionable and malleable citizenry. You just keep selling our new world to them, and we'll take care of the rest. Most will see it's a lot easier to join us than fight us."

"There will be plenty who will fight," Kahn responded.
"That's why we have the citizens' army."

CHAPTER 13

ALEJA AWOKE THE DAY after her vaccine inoculation feeling as if she'd been on a monumental drinking binge. Maria had been dozing in a chair beside her bed but came out of a partial sleep with a start when she heard her mother rousing. After many hugs, some breakfast, and a bath, Aleja felt somewhat better, though far from recovered. Nonetheless, she wanted to get back to work. Maria briefed her on the happenings and the success of the vaccine, bringing a smile to Aleja's face with the news that so many lives had been saved. She asked Maria to get her admin to set up an immediate secured conference call with the twenty key leaders of the Resistance.

On her screen, faces filled with joy at the sight of her. Aleja thanked them for their prayers and best wishes and then asked for an update.

Henry Little Hawk was the first to speak. "We have a lot of our people against this whole thing," he said. "Several of our high-tech leaders have been forced to cooperate under threat of having their families arrested and detained in camps of some kind. We don't know what those are yet. We have many calling for a total boycott of the chip implants when they come out."

The other members of the group grumbled loudly that they agreed.

The news about the threats to families shook Aleja. "Let's think this through," she said. "If we don't get the chip implants, for starters, we are probably going to get locked out of the internet. And perhaps get arrested and sent to these camps if there have already been threats about noncompliance. We can't take Kahn's word that all he wants is Phase 1 of the plan, the cybersecurity shield. He can easily move into Phase 2, the cashless digital economy, and make it mandatory to have a chip to buy anything. Our people could be starved into submission. Especially those with children. For now, we have to get the chip implants so we can continue to have internet access to communicate and trade. We can always remove the chips from our hands any time we feel we need to."

Heads nodded and the grumbling died down.

"I want you all to know that I have been talking to Jenks Kennard, Bur McAnter's former partner," Little Hawk went on. "Kennard has agreed to help us either take Sentinel over or, at worst case, shut it down. I need some time to get this going, but in the meantime, I think it's a good idea for each of us to lead rallies in our own states to comply with the law for now. We don't want to create any suspicion that we are up to something."

Nods of approval came again from all the participants.

"Does Kennard think he can actually take over Sentinel?" Aleja asked.

"If he can get Bur McAnter on our side."

"Fat chance of that," one of the other senators said. "He's a Nationalist through and through."

"Kennard knows McAnter well," Little Hawk responded. "He may be able to make him see how Sentinel is about to be exploited."

Aleja came back in. "I say we give this some time, and in the meantime, we play smart and by their rules. We'll need to quickly get the word out to our people. Many of them are still going to want to fight, and we've got to turn that around. Are we in agreement?"

"Agreed," came from all.

"And I would also recommend that Henry take over as leader of the Resistance. I am not strong enough yet."

The group agreed again.

Aleja shut down her end of the conference and fell back against her pillow. Even this small discussion had drained all the energy she had.

CHAPTER 14

BUR HAD HAD NO sleep for almost forty-eight hours as he and his teams worked to get Sentinel up and running across the internet. There had been many ups and downs, but now that the initial rebellion by the techies had been thwarted and all the access points had been updated, Bur was ready to have the device manufacturers and cable companies send Sentinel downloads to all their customers' computers, phones, and other devices. He was dragging as he entered Stanyan's office for a status meeting. Paulo Vanderhurst was already there.

Stanyan shook his head and let out a sigh. "It's been a ride," he said, handing Bur a cup of coffee. "Now we just wait for companies to tee off the downloads. Hopefully we'll be done by tomorrow night."

Bur accepted the coffee and took a big sip. "Hopefully, barring any major surprises."

Stanyan continued, "The president has given us some good news. Biosafe is on schedule for delivery of the anthrax vaccines. Therefore, he'd like us to proceed with the distribution of the chip implants ASAP. We need to get the process down cold so that there are no glitches with the vaccine distribution. Where are we on the CNID database, Bur, and the master distribution list, Paulo?"

Bur rubbed at his forehead and replied, "I've got built what I can. No medical records yet, but basic identity and commerce information on everyone in the country."

Paulo Vanderhurst gave his report. "The distribution process should be done by end of week."

"Wow!" Bur exclaimed, "That was fast. There are shitloads of distribution centers to coordinate with. They've all been contacted?"

"We've got Edgewood's whole team assigned to it," Vanderhurst replied. "He's got agents in every state and major city. Their badges seem to get them fast attention."

"Can I see the plan?" Bur said. "I am very impressed."

Vanderhurst instructed Sentinel to bring up the layout of all the schools and churches across the nation that would become distribution centers. "These designated centers will receive their shipments from the manufacturers through the post office via a shipping list managed by Sentinel," Vanderhurst said. "The product packages each have an RFID chip, which is used by Sentinel to direct each package to the appropriate distribution center. It would be really great if we could build a dynamic scheduling system that alerts everyone through their Sentinel-enabled device to be routed to the least busy center in their area for pickup. I know you're busy, but do you think you could work this in?"

Bur was about to say, "What? Are you kidding me? I'm swamped," but then changed his mind, thinking through what would be required and realizing Vanderhurst didn't have the deep working knowledge of Sentinel to handle it. "Sure, I should be able to get to it tomorrow. I see that it would be a nice feature. But let me ask you, how does Sentinel know when an implant kit is picked up?"

Vanderhurst replied, "For this initial distribution, Sentinel won't know until the microchips are implanted and activated by the user. But as soon as that happens, we'll know where each kit is and who has it. For the vaccine, since no one will be able to get it without a chip implant, the user will have to authenticate via a reader in the distribution center when he or she picks it up. We will have much tighter control of that distribution than the implants."

"I see," Bur replied. "This Sentinel master distribution list must have been quite an effort."

"Yes, I am quite proud of it," Vanderhurst said. "Let me show you something else." He had Sentinel bring up another grid overlay of the distribution centers. "We've already started making some shipments of the implants, and you can see the count as it builds in each center."

Bur leaned in closer to the screen. "I see blue dots and red dots," he said. "What's the difference between the blue and red?"

Stanyan took over the conversation for Vanderhurst. "There are two batches of chips, Bur. The red dots you're seeing are a separate group of chips for illegal immigrants, criminals, gangbangers, et cetera, that law enforcement can use for specialized tracking and surveillance."

"What the hell?" Bur said. "Whose idea was that and why am I just finding out now?"

"It was the president's idea, Bur," Stanyan replied. "All of these people are going to be initially rounded up and taken to detention centers where they'll get these implants in their butts. Kahn knows of a company that designs special air guns for giving shots and vaccines, right through your clothes. The guns were modified to shoot these chips. Any people with these chips seen outside the camps are going to get immediate attention."

"Unless these scumbags get entered into the CNID. Then we turn their chips blue," Vanderhurst said.

"And what are the requirements for them to get into the CNID?" Bur asked, very confused.

"They take a pledge to do whatever we ask them to," Vanderhurst went on. "Think of them as a new labor force. If they break the law or don't do what we ask, their chips get turned back to red, and they go back into the detention centers."

Bur shook his head, taking another big gulp of coffee. "I have not heard about the detention centers either."

Stanyan nodded and shrugged. "That's because they're new since this Iran scare. We can at any time pass into a full-scale state of emergency, and the president wants us to have camps ready for sympathizers or onshore terrorists. Anybody the army thinks fits those general descriptions will get picked up."

"The army?"

"For all practical purposes, we are at war, Bur," Stanyan went on. "This is what happens when we get attacked on our own soil."

"So they can basically throw anyone they want into a detention center?"

"No," Vanderhurst said. "Only people without a blue chip. Anybody with a blue chip is safe unless they break the law. Then their chip is turned red."

"Nice to find out stuff like this," Bur said testily. "When does all this go public?"

Stanyan shook his head. "It's not going public; it's just going to happen. Reporters will find out, but it really doesn't matter if people don't like it. Again, it's just something that has to be done when we're close to war."

"How many of these detention camps are we talking about?" Bur asked.

"Not sure," Stanyan said. "Above my pay grade. Just like you guys, I have my own status meetings with my bosses, but there's a lot I don't know. That's the way the military operates. I can see this is bothering you, Bur, but you've got to get used to it. None of us ever know all that goes on in this country. The higher up we go, the more we know, but there's also a downside to that. There's a code of operation we have to follow, whether we like it or not, and if we don't follow, there are people who make sure we do. You saw some of those tactics we had to use on the internet boys to comply. Unfortunately, it can get worse, much worse, as the stakes get higher and higher. It's something that we all need to keep in mind." He got up from his desk and stretched. "Let's get a little sleep, gentlemen, and come back at it in four hours."

CHAPTER 15

AFTER THE STATUS MEETING, Bur went back to his one-bedroom apartment on the third floor of the dormitory and plopped down on his couch facing the Pacific. After this new information from Stanyan and Vanderhurst, he had many questions that needed answers. As a lifelong programmer, he was always using logic to find his answers or solve his problems, but he'd built Sentinel to do all that for him. All his years of problem-solving algorithms had been incorporated into Sentinel through artificial intelligence and machine learning, so he didn't have to do that detailed work anymore. But until this juncture, he had never pictured just how difficult it might be for Sentinel to answer hypothetical questions. He wondered if the self-learning mechanisms he had built into it would be up to the task. He shook his head and recalled the last conversations he'd had with Jenks Kennard on this issue before he'd come to work for Stanyan.

"I want you to sit down and think for a moment what we have built here, Bur," Jenks had said to him. "We will have access to every action and event ever recorded, or in the process of being executed. Athena will know virtually everything."

"I am aware of that," Bur had responded.

"Are you? Are you really aware of that? Do you really comprehend the power Athena has if indeed she is installed on every device? You realize that with this kind of information, we can not only know everything, we can predict much of the future based on statistical analysis and probability theory. We can lay out the solutions for complex issues that would have taken months or years before. We can now apply enormous amounts of learning to predict trends and ends. This is true power."

Bur thought deeply about Jenks's statement and his warning not to join Stanyan. "There is information, prescience, and power-to-control in Athena that truly make her a god," Jenks had said, "more powerful than any other god in history. Our ancestors prayed to God for salvation, guidance, and mercy, and feared the wrath of God if they went against his canons. Athena is far more powerful, because she can reward or punish immediately to maintain her canons. Athena needs no rigid rules to follow, just desired outcomes. She will figure out how to achieve any objective and orchestrate the actions and subactions to make it happen. If we ever install Athena, the challenge that you and I will face, Bur, is to get people to trust her."

Bur came out of his recollections knowing that his Sentinel was nowhere near as powerful as Athena and did not have her power to predict and control. He had left all of that for later, once the security shield had been put in place. For now, Sentinel still needed detailed instructions, and there was no intent-based analysis to judge one man's actions compared to another's. To account for these shortcomings, he had built a secret back door into Sentinel that would allow him to take it over should he see it was being abused.

Now seeing the need to use his back door, he used his secret sign-on, AIPOTU—UTOPIA reversed—whose presence and actions could not be recorded or traced. He interacted with Sentinel through AIPOTU by keyboard rather than voice, so there was no possibility of being overheard. *Find out about the attacks on Los Angeles. Who was involved and what they did.*

Sentinel replied on his screen, *Please provide an actor or actors from which to start.*

Bur thought back on the conversation with Stanyan just now. *Use General Stanyan, Paulo Vanderhurst, and President Kahn.*

Affirmative.

Bur's screen filled with avatar gods accessing deep mines, which he had enjoyed building to represent Sentinel's data mining capabilities. At this point, Sentinel had access to every piece of information on the hundreds of millions of computers, laptops, and phones on which it had been installed in the country. Twenty minutes passed and Bur wondered if the question was too much for the supermachine, but then his screen filled with a report.

An encrypted videoconference took place on the day of the attack, initiated by Kahn to Stanyan and Vanderhurst, but it included two other actors: Director Shaw of the CDC and Roger Edgewood of the CIA. The communications of each of these five actors were then traced back through the preceding six months to determine who else may have been in their fields of influence, and what other actions may have impacted them. A key event took place in October at the Buenos Aires World Summit that appears to be the starting point for these overlapping actors and their communications. Attendees at that summit included President Kahn, Balto Nitup of Russia, Mohammad bin Qatmah of Saudi Arabia, Recep Tayyip Nagore of Turkey, and Ariel Levy of Israel. Logs from CIA satellite listeners of the key attendees of this conference show them meeting with the secondary actors:

Edgewood, Shaw, General Herman Lancaster, army chief of staff; Anton Olderian, the president of Biosafe; Victor Blodskoff of Russian intelligence; Omar Zensar of the Saudi Arabia Royal Guard; Emin Yavuz of the Turkish MIT; Asher Dahan of the Israeli Mossad; General Alex Stanyan, director of the CCC; and Paulo Vanderhurst, chief architect of the CCC.

Two separate themes emerged from these subsequent meetings. First, the DWP cyberattack, and second, the anthrax attack. Regarding the cyberattack, two days after the Buenos Aires summit, President Kahn initiated a videoconference over a government network with General Stanyan and Paulo Vanderhurst. Transcript embedded. The next day, General Stanyan and Vanderhurst initiated a call to Russia to Victor Blodskoff of Russian intelligence. Two days later, General Stanyan received a call from Blodskoff in Iran, on that same number. Over the course of the next six weeks, ten additional calls were held between Stanyan, Vanderhurst, Edgewood, and Blodskoff on that number in Iran. On the day of the attacks in Los Angeles, a text message claiming responsibility for the attack came from that same number in Iran. Stanyan and Edgewood spoke to Blodskoff moments after that text message on that same number.

As for the anthrax attack, six secondary actors met twice in Berlin at the Biosafe labs. After the first of those Berlin meetings, Shaw, Edgewood, and Vanderhurst met at the CDC headquarters in Atlanta. There are no notes or recordings from those meetings specifically, but after that meeting, Edgewood called Olderian at Biosafe:

"Good evening, Anton, I hope you are well."

"Getting better every day, Roger, thanks for asking. The new medication is working wonders, and my doctors tell me I should be well by end of next week. And how are you feeling?"

"Very well. I started work on my new home yesterday and should be finished by end of this week. I would love for you to see

it. *Hopefully you will be well enough to travel. I want to keep our bet that we have bigger bass in Virginia than you do in Berlin."*

"Wouldn't miss it for the world. I will warn you; I am an expert fisherman. I only go after really big fish."

"We have the biggest in the country. I have been to every other state and know for certain."

Bur scrolled through the rest of the conversation but was too tired to take in all the detail. *How do these meetings with Biosafe relate to the LA attack?* he asked Sentinel.

A shipment of one hundred cartons left Biosafe two days before the LA attack. They were delivered to a warehouse in downtown Los Angeles, from which Edgewood made a call back to Olderian at Biosafe on the same day. Edgewood then had an encrypted group chat with fifty persons, listed below. All of them are members or former members of military intelligence, CIA, or other special operations. From their phone and text messages, they visited the warehouse in Los Angeles where Edgewood was on the day before the attack. They were also on the streets of Los Angeles during the attack. Another group chat went out at the same time the DWP was attacked: "Go."

Bur jumped to the end of the report and read the conclusion.

...a much broader attack is planned.

Bur stopped reading and saved the report to his private cloud. He found the card Senator Trujillo had given him at the DWP and dialed the number through Sentinel. *Senator, this is Bur McAnter,* he typed. It went through text-to-voice translation for the senator.

"Dr. McAnter, I am so glad you called. What can I do for you?"

Bur was paranoid that Vanderhurst or Stanyan would knock on his door. He calmed himself with the knowledge that as long as he was in AIPOTU, this call, like the queries he had just run, would not exist in any logs. *You okay to turn on your cam? Would like to see you f to f.*

"Yes. I'd like that," she replied. Her image popped up on his screen.

Bur was shocked at how pale and gaunt she looked. *How r you?*

"Better, thank you. The new vaccine helped. Still have a way to go, though."

So sorry for you and the rest in LA. B4 we begin, need your word this is between you and me only.

"You have my word, Doctor."

And if any of this gets out, you need to get my family to safety.

"You have my word, Doctor. Why is it you called?"

I have just learned about a second set of chip implants for so-called lawbreakers that will be put in detention camps. Do you about this?

"I have heard about the detention camps that Kahn described to threaten the internet providers, but not the chips."

Okay, suspected so. I got curious what else might be going on. Just had Sentinel run a report.

She coughed on the other end of the line. "Go on."

I believe Kahn was behind the attacks—cyber and anthrax—working with foreign actors. He may have plans for further attacks.

"Oh my God, Dr. McAnter!" she gasped, and broke out in another fit of coughing. "That is hard to believe, even for Kahn. What evidence do you have?"

Bur took a deep breath and gave her a summary of the details Sentinel had presented. *If we take this public, many would disagree because it comes from a computer...no corroborating evidence from humans.*

"You are right about that, Doctor," the senator respond-ed. "And it is hard to believe that Kahn would initiate such an attack on his own country. These charges are so severe that without more proof, Kahn could easily accuse the Resistance of setting this up to make him look bad, or worse, to take over the country. He could even fabricate some of his own ev-idence that you yourself are working with foreign actors to carry out a coup."

Bur paused, thinking through what she had said. *Yes. I'd be arrested. No option for additional info from Sen if that happens. We need more reports.*

"Doctor, you have me appropriately terrified. If you can't convince people that this is going to happen, can it happen? Is this a threat that Sentinel is hypothesizing, or is it really possible?"

Bur rubbed his eyes. *For sure. Sen will be on every device in the country. Kahn can use it to control the news—and truth.*

She went into another coughing jag, making Bur feel even more desperate. "We somehow have to bring Sentinel down, then," she said, when her coughing subsided. "Could you bring it down and say that it failed, had a fatal flaw—something like that?"

Bur thought through how he could do that. *NO. Need to expose rest of actors and learn full plan.*

"So what are you proposing?" the senator asked. "And let me tell you in advance that I cannot simply keep this informa-tion to myself, despite the promise I made to you earlier, now that I know about it."

Understand. We have to take this public—sometime—but need more evidence.

"And how would we get that?"

Bur looked through Sentinel's report again. *More reports. And a backup plan for me, if I'm caught.*

"Doctor, from what you've just told me, we are already dealing with treason from the LA attack, and the possibility of further treason on a much larger scale, which are adequate grounds for my colleagues in the House and Senate to start immediate investigations. We can ensure both your and your family's safety."

Yes, but then I'd have to leave here—we'd lose access to Sen. According to the Constitution, treason requires a confession or testimony from two witnesses. Sen and I are only witnesses. Doubt that will fly. Need more evidence of Kahn's intent.

"So what are you proposing, Doctor?"

"Sen is key. We need to ensure we can keep control of it. I need help from someone on the outside who understands Sen."

"Do you have someone in mind?"

Jenks Kennard. We built Athena together, predecessor of Sen. Not on good terms with him though.

The senator gasped and a smile broke out on her face. "Doctor, that might be more possible than you think. Senator Little Hawk grew up with Jenks Kennard in South Dakota. He contacted him after the attack to see if there was a way he could take Sentinel down if necessary. Perhaps Henry can help facilitate a call with Kennard."

Bur wiped at his eyes, fearing this was too good to be true. *He doesn't like what I've done with Sen. Not fond of politics either.*

"Can I try to get Senator Little Hawk on this call now?" the senator asked. "There's no time to delay."

Bur looked at his clock to see how much time he had before he had to meet with Stanyan and Vanderhurst again. *Yes, let's try, but I'm short on time.*

"I'll patch the senator in."

Bur waited anxiously as she put him on hold. He had very mixed feelings about working with Jenks again but knew it was his only option.

"Dr. McAnter?" Senator Trujillo said, her live image reappearing on Bur's on screen. "I have Senator Little Hawk on the line. Dr. Kennard is with him at Crazy Horse. I am going to leave it up to you to brief them."

"Hello, Doctor, this is Henry Little Hawk." The senator came up on Bur's screen.

Then Jenks appeared. "Hello, Bur."

Jenks? Bur typed, gazing at his old friend. He froze momentarily, not sure how to continue. *How r you?*

There was a pause. "I'm okay, Bur. You have a change of mind?"

Bur's fingers fumbled for the keys as he responded. *Yes. I was wrong about Kahn. I'm sorry. Need your help to stop him.* Bur gave him a brief rundown of what he'd told Senator Trujillo. *Would like to dup Sen to another cloud. Need much more info that I don't have time to run here. And if they catch me, need to pass control over to you.*

Another pause on the other end. "Why me, Bur?"

BC, I trust you. YR the only one who can help me out of this mess.

"But can I trust you?" Jenks responded. "If I help you, we go back to Athena."

You can trust me, Jenks. We go back to Athena.

"Okay," Jenks said, nodding to him over his monitor. "What do we need to do."

I have a back door to Sen. Need to get you auth'd so you can op Sen w/o detection and cloak your calls and actions. But you need direct handoff from me first. Bur paused, staring at the words he just wrote. The thought of handing off his creation bothered him deeply on one level but gave him a sense of re-lief on another.

"I assume that everyone who is currently using Sentinel will just go about their business as usual once this is done?" Jenks asked.

They won't have a clue. Forgot to ask—you have a DC?

Senator Little Hawk came in. "We can use the data center here on the campus at Crazy Horse. We are state of the art."

"What about the authentication canons?" Jenks asked. "Will we both need to sign on every day to prevent the dead man's switch from shutting down the system?"

Yes. That may be all that can save me. Let's get started. Bur authenticated into AIPOTU with facial and iris scans. *Grant Jenks Kennard access to the master.*

Sentinel responded, *Capturing his facial image and iris scan now. Authenticated.*

One more thing, Sentinel. Remove my rights to grant any other access to the master. Only Jenks now.

Affirmative.

Bur's momentary sense of relief disappeared as the full weight of what he had just done sunk in on him. His hands shook as he continued to type. *Clone Sentinel to the Crazy Horse Data Center. Give it access to all resources here at Eagle's Cliff and share the load between the two. Intercept any sur-veillance attempts on Resistance Party members of Congress, Jenks, and my family.*

Affirmative.

Bur stared back at the other three on the videoconfer-ence. *Please get my family to safety.* He keyed in his family's address in San Francisco. *Senator Trujillo, please go personal-ly for her. We can't risk spreading this info outside this call. Call me when you get there. Good luck, Jenks. Need to sign off now.*

Bur switched off his console and sat back in his chair, totally exhausted. He tried to think of any way that Stanyan or Vanderhurst could find out what he'd just done, but he was too tired to concentrate and fell fast asleep.

CHAPTER 16

ALEJA THOUGHT THROUGH HER best approach. It was helpful that Sentinel could cloak Carmen McAnter's phone calls, but she suspected that Kahn had other forms of surveillance on her and other Resistance leaders outside of Sentinel. She had to assume that at some point, Kahn would find Mrs. McAnter, so then it would be a question of what would happen. Her best option, she deduced, was to have the McAnters on her own turf, where she could move them around rapidly if necessary, and in the event Kahn wanted to try to use force to take her, she would have plenty of armed Resistance at her disposal. While armed confrontation was not something she wanted, keeping Mrs. McAnter and her kids safe was vital if she wanted Bur's help exposing Kahn's plot.

She contacted several of her Resistance precinct leaders and established four safe houses among which she could rotate the McAnters to keep their location dynamic. She also dialed up a dozen of her and her husband's ex-SEAL mates to lead and manage other armed Resistance in her area to form a shift of guards who would communicate on walkie-talkies to call in reinforcements if necessary. She was counting on Kahn not to use force, knowing that it could trigger a much larger confrontation. She'd considered trying to get the McAnters out of the country, but once outside her own turf, she knew Kahn had a huge advantage over her.

After setting up the basic structure of the plan, she arranged to be flown out of the Santa Monica Airport to SFO on a private plane owned by one of her Resistance associates. This allowed her the fastest route to San Francisco with the least possibility of detection. Although she was still extremely tired and weak from her anthrax exposure, she boosted her energy with her most tried and tested aid: black coffee.

A Resistance SUV picked her up at SFO and drove her to the Haight-Ashbury district. The McAnters' flat lay in a diverse neighborhood of the lower Haight, in a row of old Victorians. Aleja and her guard moved rapidly up to the front door, not wanting to be seen by the neighbors, even though it was 3:00 a.m.

Carmen McAnter seemed near panic when she opened the door. Long auburn hair, light green eyes, freckled face. She was a striking woman, despite the worry lines around her eyes and temples.

"Mrs. McAnter, I am here at the request of your husband," Aleja said to her with as much calm as she could muster. "Please call him. He is expecting your call. He will explain to you why we're here. If we may come in?"

"Senator Trujillo?" Carmen said, sounding confused to see her. She nodded for her to come in and closed the door quickly behind her and her guard. Aleja had her guard check the room for bugs and set up a scrambler so that if there were any remote probes, they'd get nothing but static. She couldn't help but notice the many pictures of Carmen and Bur with their two children placed around the small but cozy flat.

Carmen videoconferenced Bur and turned on her speakerphone when his image came up.

"Hello, baby," Bur said.

"What's going on, Bur?" she responded nervously.

"It is important that you and the kids leave with Senator Trujillo right now," Bur said. "I have uncovered national security information that I must make public, but I have to know you and the kids are safe first."

"What are you talking about?" Carmen said desperately. Beads of sweat formed on her upper lip.

"I don't have time to discuss it with you now, baby. Just know that Senator Trujillo will keep you safe. As soon as I can confirm that she has you in a safe place, I will leave Eagle's Cliff and join you."

"Bur, I'm scared."

"I understand," Bur replied. "I am too. But we have to trust the senator and the Resistance. I have been wrong all along about Kahn."

Carmen broke out in tears, which brought her five-year-old son and three-year-old daughter from the corner they'd been hiding in.

"You leave my momma alone!" the boy said, leaping between Aleja and his mother.

Aleja looked down and saw the fire in the little boy's eyes. "I'm not here to hurt your mother, son."

"You'd better not. Since my daddy's gone, I'm the man of the house. You get outta here right now."

She watched him tremble and felt embarrassed to have frightened him. He held one arm in front of his mother, and the other in front of his little sister, protecting them. "I'm warning you," the boy said, stuttering.

"It's okay, son," Bur said over the speakerphone. "She is there to help you. I want you, Mommy, and Gen to go with her. I will meet you as soon as I can."

"Where we going?" Genny called out.

Aleja reached down to calm her. "It's going to be okay, honey. I can't imagine how this appears to you, but I am going to help you and your dad." Then standing up to speak to Carmen again, she said, "I'd like you to come back to Venice with me. You'll be much safer there, and it will give your husband the peace of mind to do what he needs to do. I'm sorry that I can't tell you more right now, but we must get going. We cannot risk being seen here. Can you get dressed and pack some quick bags for your kids? I have plenty of clothes that would fit you."

"What about Malcolm?" Jimmy asked, putting his arm around the big collie's neck.

"He can come too," Aleja responded. "I have many friends with dogs that he can stay with and play. It'll be best if we keep him safe for you until we get your dad and then you can all get back together again."

Carmen looked down at her kids and nodded. "We may have to move around in a hurry and stay quiet. He's not so good at that."

Aleja let out a deep breath and helped with the bags. Ten minutes later, they were back in the SUV and on their way to SFO. She fought to stay awake and keep up her strength, not wanting to show any signs of weakness that would spook Mrs. McAnter and her children.

CHAPTER 17

JENKS HAD BEEN RUNNING reports on Sentinel since Sentinel had been cloned over to the Crazy Horse Data Center. With the information he had just uncovered, he knew it was time to assemble the others.

Jenks rounded up Henry and Madelena from the main living quarters at Crazy Horse and set up a videoconference with Aleja. "Thank you all for joining," he said. "I have new information."

"Before we begin," Henry said, "how are you, Aleja? And how is Mrs. McAnter?"

"I'm tired but better," she said, holding back a cough. "I hope you don't mind that my daughter is on the call. She's my backup."

The others all laughed. "No problem," Henry responded. "Good morning, Maria."

"Good morning, Senator," the teenager answered, frowning.

"She trying to get me to rest more," Aleja said, seeing her daughter's expression. "As for Mrs. McAnter, she is terrified for her children and her husband. I just want to make sure her call to him last night was not traced."

"Your calls and hers are all cloaked by AIPOTU," Jenks responded. "Incoming and outgoing calls will not appear in Sentinel's records. Any incoming calls will go immediately to your voice mails. You can then answer them as you wish; however, there will be no record of them. So, for instance, if Kahn were to call you just to ask how you're doing, and then ask his team to trace the call so he could find out where you were, there would be no trace in Sentinel. This the downside of cloaking, but a low probability at this point, in my opinion."

"Is there any other way for them to find me or Mrs. McAnter?" Aleja asked.

"Sentinel has a new fleet of surveillance satellites that are able to pick up digitized images from the thousands of surveillance cameras around the country. Through AI, it creates video analytics and looks for behavior patterns that may indicate abnormal behavior. Sentinel can then create a facial scan and last known location for individuals it does not have in its database after the biochip implants. A second new technology, laser microphones, are being rapidly set up along with the surveillance cameras. The microphones provide a secondary surveillance capability—they will be able to penetrate buildings to capture the sonar waves of voice conversations. The waves are then digitized by voice recognition technology to capture the entire conversation as well as to create a voice-print, which can then be used to quickly identify subsequent conversations by that person."

"Which means they can find her no matter what," Aleja said.

Jenks nodded. "The overriding principle of the security shield is to know who everyone in the country is. All the combined data from the chip implants, video, and audio surveillance is captured by Sentinel and turned into knowledge. This information is stored for every moment of every day to create a digital history of the nation. With that digital history, Sentinel can analyze and predict anyone's activities for any period of time. And specifically, for those without biochip implants, Sentinel can send facial scans and voiceprints out to law enforcement, along with their last sighted location. It is virtually impossible to be anonymous in our country now."

"Which means we must move fast," Henry said.

"Yes," Jenks answered. "And that brings us back to the original purpose of my call." Turning back to his monitor, he said, "Sentinel, please present the latest report you just ran."

Sentinel created a written summary for them on the screen, which it went over verbally. "Biosafe, the company Kahn just bought to create the anthrax vaccines, has been experimenting with creating different strains of anthrax that are resilient to current vaccines and antibiotics. It now has created a deadly strain which it can mass produce in nasal sprays, and it has a vaccine, also in a nasal spray, that can neutralize it. This is an initiative sponsored by a secret alliance called the Pure World Coalition. Its members in addition to the United States include Russia, Saudi Arabia, Israel, and Turkey."

"What is their objective?" Henry said.

"They use the term 'racial cleansing' in many of their communications," Sentinel responded. "From Kahn's regular contact with these ultra-rightists, their objective appears to be to use the new strain of anthrax to cleanse the country, and perhaps the world, of what they consider to be inferior races."

"But why send out the vaccine to everyone in the country?" Aleja asked.

"Two distribution lists are being developed by Paulo Vanderhurst at Eagle's Cliff," Sentinel answered. "One appears to be for the Resistance and people of color, and the other for the Nationalists. The nasal sprays are being manufactured in two separate facilities: the vaccines in Russia and the live anthrax sprays in Berlin. The Berlin shipments are to go to the Resistance and the Russian shipments to the Nationalists."

Aleja gasped and looked at the others. "He can't be that crazy," she said, and started to cough again.

"That's what most people would think if we were to take any of this public," Henry responded.

"We will need proof of what's coming out of Berlin," Aleja said. "Once we have that and McAnter, we can go public."

"Agreed," Jenks said. "But there is still one key piece of information we need. Sentinel, can you tell us when Kahn is planning to do the cleansing distribution?"

Sentinel replied, "There are a number of references to a 'D-Day' which is dependent upon the outcome of the distribution of the chip implant kits. There are several references that imply it will be within weeks, but no specific date."

Aleja sipped at her coffee pensively. "Sooner than I thought. Do you know if any of the actual anthrax has shipped yet from Berlin?"

After a short pause, Sentinel replied, "There are no records of any shipments after the smoke canisters that were used in the LA attack."

"So we'll need to go to Germany, then," Aleja responded. "I will lead this mission."

"What?" Maria responded. "Like hell you will. You can barely walk by yourself, let alone lead a dangerous mission. And you sure as hell can't take the risk of being detected."

"I will be as good as new by tomorrow," Aleja replied. "And I will work out a plan that will be low risk."

"Fat chance of that," Maria rejoindered.

"I agree with Maria," Henry came in. "Our whole mission would be jeopardized, and McAnter would be in immediate danger if you were detected in a covert operation. Why don't we get our military contacts to handle this? They have plenty of embedded agents in Germany."

Aleja shook her head. "Too many moving parts for a mission like this right now. Besides, it doesn't have to be covert. It can be right out in the open. I can go in under the pretense that I am making an inspection tour for Congress, just to see how things are going. Once I see the lay of the land there, a plan will come to me. All I need is a few of my old SEAL team who can think on their feet."

"What kind of a plan is that?" Maria fumed.

"Trust me, we are good."

"So good you ended up in a Venezuelan prison for six months?"

Aleja bristled. "My team and I were set up through an intelligence leak. That's why I want to lead this with people I know."

Henry came back into the conversation. "You are much more important to the Resistance here, Aleja," he said. "If you somehow manage to get yourself killed or captured, we will have a major setback."

Aleja shook her head forcefully. "If we don't get those samples and prove this conspiracy, our people are going to war. This is the most important mission we have right now, and I am the right person for the job."

Maria grabbed both of her mother's hands in hers. "I'm going with you then," she said firmly. "You've taught me to shoot, and Dad taught me hand-to-hand combat. I'm a second-degree black belt, for God's sake. On top of that, I speak German from Dad, which you don't."

Aleja started to object, but Maria pressed harder on her hands. "I can take you in your condition, and dammit, I will tie you up if I have to. Either I go or you don't."

Aleja thought back to her husband and how much he loved his daughter. She wondered what he would say about this.

"I can read your mind," Maria said. "Dad would want me to go to protect you from this half-baked idea. He knows I'm good. And, after all, I am your daughter."

"For sure, Maria can't go," Henry said, "even though I am warming up to your idea, Aleja."

Maria slammed her fist down on the table. "I am a part of the Resistance, dammit!" she shouted. "I want to do my part and fight for our cause. You are going to need young leaders in order to win. You think we are all just going to go back to high school if a war breaks out? Let me prove myself."

Aleja cut Henry off before he could speak again. "I know her better than you, Henry. I think she could take me. And besides, having her with me will help make this more personal for the public. She goes."

Maria shook her head in surprise, then smiled broadly at the whole group. "I won't let you down," she said, breathing hard. "Nobody is going to mess with my mother."

Aleja gave her another big hug, then said to Henry, "You are only an hour's drive from General Bascom at Ellsworth, and you know each other well. Can you bring him up to speed and have him help me get in and out of Berlin? I'll concentrate on pulling my SEAL team together."

"Will do," Henry said. "Godspeed."

CHAPTER 18

CARMEN MCANTER WALKED THROUGH the crowded streets of Venice in the late afternoon on her way to a new Resistance safe house. She and her kids had got into Santa Monica at 7:00 a.m. and slept at their initial safe house throughout the morning and most of the afternoon. She carried Genevieve in her arms, and one of the Resistance guards carried Jimmy. Two more guards accompanied them in front and behind, hidden in the crowds. The senator had given her a Dodgers cap to help her blend in.

A fog was just starting to roll in over the ocean, bringing back memories of the magical years when she and Bur had first met. She knew she should focus on the moment, but her mind forced her into the past, when she and Bur had experienced better days. They'd both grown up poor in the Haight. Bur's father died when he was twelve, leaving his mother to raise him on a schoolteacher's salary. He'd worked for a moving company after school and on weekends to help pay the bills. He met Carmen one afternoon when some homeless men had cornered her on her way home from high school. He stepped in and drove them off, then asked her to come to his flat for a cup of tea to calm her nerves. Raspberry Royale. It was still her favorite.

The flat was empty while his mother was away teaching, and their relationship grew. They soon became lovers. Bur began to tell her his dreams on those afternoons. They spent hours, before he had to go to work at the moving company, visualizing what they would do when they grew up. He dreamed of a utopia where everyone had a job, a purpose, and a good place to live without fear. Carmen wanted a big house on the bay with lots of kids.

Bur had excelled in mathematics and was confident he could find the answer to any problem. He was so good that by sixteen he'd graduated from high school and been offered scholarships to a dozen universities. He chose Cornell mainly because he wanted to see the East Coast, but he didn't want to go alone. Carmen smiled as she remembered him telling her that she was coming with him wherever he went. He promised that someday, he'd take her to the moon.

He'd convinced her mom he'd make a great life for her. Carmen had four sisters and a missing father, so her mother didn't object. It wouldn't have mattered anyway; Carmen would have gone with him no matter what. Bur's mother had been a different story. She wasn't happy at all about him moving to the East Coast and had begged him to at least go to Stanford, but his mind was made up. Carmen remembered Bur's mother pulling her aside and telling her to keep him in line. Carmen recalled the numerous times Bur had been called into the principal's office for fighting. He had developed a reputation for protecting the nerds in his school from gangs and bullies. Carmen smiled inside as she remembered the "family" of misfits and weaklings who followed him around like a hero.

Carmen and Bur had been married in the summer of their seventeenth birthdays with both parents' consent and the local court's approval. They traveled by bus to Ithaca just in time for the opening term at Cornell. She gladly worked at McDonald's to help meet the expenses his scholarship didn't cover, and he worked as a house painter. Regardless of the length of their days, he was never tired when he came home to her. One look into his deep green eyes, one touch of his strong but gentle hands, and she was stirred to go on, no matter what obstacles they faced.

He'd obtained his bachelor of science within two years at Cornell and began working on his PhD at nineteen. He wrote his thesis on neural networks and artificial intelligence at age twenty-one and went on to build Athena with Jenks Kennard. She had fond memories of Jenks. He and Bur had spent much of their time together, often so wrapped in their work that Carmen would have to bring food to campus or they would forget to eat. But when Alex Stanyan had offered them both a job to build Athena for the government, Bur and Jenks parted company on bad terms. Bur took Stanyan's offer and moved back to the Bay Area, while Jenks stayed in Ithaca. Carmen wondered where they'd be right now if the two friends had stayed together at Cornell. Bur had never been comfortable with his decision to split with Jenks but had fallen under Kahn's spell, as so many in the nation had.

She came out of her memories as she and her kids arrived at the new safe house. It was an apartment above a tattoo parlor. Her guards escorted her into the apartment, called the senator to tell her that their wards were safe, and then stayed outside her door.

She inspected the apartment. There was a single bedroom with two double beds, one bathroom with a shower, and a small kitchen with a well-stocked refrigerator. The living room had a big picture window, but the curtains had been drawn, and the guards had told her not to open them. At the back of the apartment was another window that opened onto a fire escape above an alley. She plopped down on the couch with her kids and chomped on an apple from the basket of fruit on the end table.

"Mommy, I'm tired. When can we go back to bed?" Genevieve asked.

"In just a minute," she said. "Just let me make sure Daddy hasn't called." She checked her cell phone again, making sure her battery was fully charged, but there were no messages or missed calls.

"Mommy, when are we going home?" Genevieve continued.

"Soon, honey, very soon."

"Okay, Mommy," Genevieve whimpered, cuddling up to her.

Carmen didn't like the sound of her girl's voice. Genevieve was answering the way she answered when she knew Carmen was lying to her. Especially when Carmen tried to tell her how long Daddy would be away from home.

"Honey," she said, bending down to eye level with Genevieve and pulling Jimmy in close, "Daddy knows something that some bad men don't want him to tell. He's going to get away from them. That's why we're here, so he can join us."

The children stared at her with shock and fear, but she felt better for finally having told them the truth. "If they come for us," she added, "I want to be prepared. Under no circumstances can we let them take us."

"No way," Jimmy said, trying to deepen his voice. He gritted his teeth and made his tiny hands into fists.

Carmen's throat closed. So much like his father. "Daddy will make everything okay," she said.

"Will the men come for us when we go home?" Genevieve asked.

The thought unsettled Carmen. "We're not going home till we get Daddy back. We've got to be ready for them here."

Genevieve jutted out her lower lip and nodded bravely, trying to shut off her tears. Jimmy put his arm around her to comfort her.

"First of all, we need a code word," Carmen said, trying to give them something to keep their minds occupied. "It will be like a game. If any one of us says the word, that means we stop everything we're doing, no matter what's happening, and immediately begin our plan of action."

The children both stared at her, saying nothing.

"Blue fish. How's that?" she said.

Jimmy shook his head. "That sounds kinda dumb."

"Okay, you think of a code word."

"Shark attack," he said.

Carmen smiled. "Okay, shark attack." She began walking around the kitchen, looking at weapons. There were no rolling pins, and the knives were too small to do much good. Then she saw the can of wasp spray. She held it out to Genevieve. "This will be your weapon. If any one of us calls the code word, you get this and spray anybody we don't know. Got it?"

Genevieve looked at the can and nodded. "That stuff poison?"

"We want to protect ourselves," Carmen answered, nodding. "They may try to hurt us. We'll have to hurt them."

Genevieve's glance darted toward the door, then back. "Okay, Mommy."

Searching further, Carmen found a broom. Handing it to Jimmy, she said, "This is a good weapon for poking." She demonstrated with a jab in the air at an imaginary assailant. "Right in the face or the throat. One good shot is all you need. Try it."

He took the broom from her and got the feel of it. "I know what to do," he said seriously.

She brushed away tears of pride, fighting to let her anger carry her through this craziness without thinking about what she was teaching her kids.

"Mommy, here's something for you," Genevieve said, moving over to the small dining table. It had a single antique candlestick that appeared to be made of lead.

"Can I have that instead, Mommy?" Jimmy said. "It's more my size. You'd be better with the broom."

Carmen held back a smile and nodded pensively. "I agree. You're better off staying low with this." She took the candlestick from Genevieve and checked its weight. Surprised by how heavy it was, she gave it to Jimmy. "Go for the groin. You understand?"

"The balls." Jimmy giggled.

Genevieve looked at him with disgust. "I know what the groind is." She always added a D to the end of that word, no matter how many times Jimmy told her the right pronunciation.

Carmen checked the apartment again, inspecting the one small window above the shower and another behind the beds. Neither opened wide enough for anyone to get through. Just the front door to worry about. "If anyone comes through the front door, we separate. We come at them from both sides. And if I tell you to run, you do as I say. Climb out the window and take the fire escape down to the alley. Then run as fast as you can."

"What about you, Mommy?" Jimmy said, eying the front door.

"I'll be right behind you, but don't wait for me. Remember, we are much better separated."

"But first we fight. Right, Mommy? Like Daddy would."

"Right," she said to the children, "but just long enough to get free."

She wished with all her might that Bur would come through those doors and end this madness. Or that he would stop Stanyan and his men before they could come after her and her kids. She quickly pushed away the thought of how Bur would react. She was afraid of the violence that was building inside her.

She heard a knock on the front door and approached it carefully, putting her finger to her lips and signaling to the children to take their weapons. "Who is it?" she said, trying to keep her voice from shaking.

"It's me, Mrs. McAnter, Aleja. May I come in?"

Carmen shooed her kids into the bedroom and opened the door.

Aleja came in and gave her a long hug. "Have you heard from your husband?"

Carmen held onto her, needing to feel safe. "No."

Aleja moved away slightly so she could look into her eyes. "I'm afraid the next step is going to have to come from him."

"Can't you go up to Eagle's Cliff to get him?"

"Not so easy. It's a secured facility. We're still working on a plan."

Carmen stared at her, face red, trembling from head to toe. Tears prevented what she was about to say.

Aleja reached out to touch her. "It's going to be okay. I can't imagine what you must be going through right now, but I am going to help you."

"What will they do with him if they find out what he's told you?"

"You can't worry about that. You'll be safe here, which will be one less thing for him to worry about while he makes his next move. And from now on, open this door to no one unless they give you the password: freedom."

Carmen sat down on the couch, holding her hands to her head, and prayed to God to please let her hear from Bur.

CHAPTER 19

HENRY LITTLE HAWK MULLED over the events of the past twenty-four hours as he entered the office of General Bobby Bascom at Ellsworth Air Force Base outside Rapid City, fifty miles northeast of Crazy Horse. Henry and General Bascom had become friends after working together on several appropriations bills on the Defense Committee. They were also both from South Dakota and committed to helping their home state, each in his own way. While Bascom was not a part of the Resistance, Henry knew him to be an honest man who would keep his word.

After shielding his ears from the passing of two F-16s, he told the general about Bur McAnter and the Sentinel reports.

Bascom's eyes narrowed and his face tightened. "How accurate do you think this information is, coming from either McAnter or Sentinel? He have any axes to grind?"

"Not that I know of," Henry responded. "He's been a Kahn supporter up till now."

"I always knew that son of a bitch was dangerous, but this is a whole new arena."

"I'm here to ask for your help to stop him."

Bascom nodded, holding Henry's eye without blinking. "You have it. I'll see the bastard hang for this." He walked to the window and looked out onto his very busy air base, still nodding his head. "With Sentinel installed everywhere now, he must feel he has one hell of a foolproof plan. What do you want me to do?"

"First of all, Senator Trujillo is going to Germany to get samples of the hot anthrax spray. She is going in on official congressional business, and a separate ex-SEAL team will go with her, but I'm worried about her running into trouble over there. We obviously can't have her captured."

Bascom smiled and said, "The Serpent? Why am I not surprised? You want me to back her up?"

Henry nodded. "Primarily to get her out if she runs into trouble."

Bascom rubbed at his chin, thinking. "Admiral Abrams should be briefed on this also, Henry. He can be trusted. If you're running a SEAL mission, active or not, he's going to want to be involved. My boys can do the flying, but he's got the Black Ops guys. Besides, we're going to need him anyway, if I'm reading what you're going to say next."

"I do want to be prepared for a takeover if for some reason we can't get the proof in time to present it to Congress and the public."

Bascom took in a deep breath and paced around his office. "Assuming we can get Admiral Abrams on board, that would put the air force and navy against the army. General Lancaster is solidly in Kahn's corner. I really don't want the military fighting itself."

Henry paused as the giant engines of an F-16 roared on takeoff. "I'm hoping we can turn the army at a grassroots level. If you and Admiral Abrams were to select your personal cadres, then each of them selects their own, etcetera, etcetera, at some point, some of your people would be bound to cross over into the army with people they know."

Bascom rubbed at his forehead. "Need to think about that one for a while, Henry, but I get your point. The only problem I see is that everyone is going to want to see this proof, whether they're in the military or not. The sooner we can get the hot anthrax sample, the better."

"It's a catch-22," Henry responded. "We can't get it back to this country and keep Senator Trujillo protected without your help. I believe you will need to solidify your commanders behind you based upon the Sentinel reports we have."

"If we're talking high treason, here, which we apparently are, we'll need her and her team to be wearing cameras and mics so we can have a clear chain of custody of the vaccine samples when she gets them out."

"Agreed," Henry said, "but the evidence is no good if we can't keep Senator Trujillo and Bur McAnter alive."

"I'll talk to Admiral Abrams and my command staff," Bascom relied. "I'll get back to you by tomorrow."

"Thank you, General," Henry said, extending his hand. "To saving the country."

CHAPTER 20

ALEJA MADE THE CALL to President Kahn, knowing that this would be the most important call of her life.

The president took her call immediately. "So good to hear from you!" he said. "How are you feeling?"

"Much better, thanks, sir. The new vaccine had a huge impact. I wanted to thank you personally for getting it to me."

"You are very welcome. Nothing could have made me happier than to hear those words from you."

"I want to return the favor by doing something substantial to help sell the whole notion of the Biosafe operation. What would you think if I made a trip to Berlin to visit the plant and thank them personally? If our people could see the operation and hear the voices of our vaccine supplier, it may go a long way toward getting the Resistance behind it. There are still many on my side who think it's all a ruse."

"What a fantastic offer!" Kahn responded. "We can show that we are working together for the health and safety of our country. Perhaps I should go with you."

Aleja had run through this scenario in her head, and while it had some upsides, it could also prevent her from completing her mission. "That is a very gracious offer with many benefits, but also a few drawbacks. I was thinking of announcing this in advance, so our country and media are prepared to do full coverage. In the current state of tension with Iran, it may not be safe to broadcast that you are there. I would be willing to bet that our generals would be against it as well. Especially if for any reason hostilities expanded and you are needed in Washington to ensure the safety of our country. One suggestion might be for you and I to hold a joint press conference showing our solidarity. You could announce that you've asked me to lead an inspection delegation to confirm progress of the vaccine development."

Kahn paused for a moment, then said, "Exceptional idea! How soon could we hold the press conference?"

Aleja's first response was, *Yes! I've lured him in*, but then something told her it had all been too easy. It could just be a case of confusion in her mind, though, lingering from the anthrax infection. In any event, she had to take what she'd been given. "I could leave this afternoon for Washington, hold the press conference with you tomorrow morning, then go directly to Berlin from there."

"Capital idea," Kahn responded. "I will start making arrangements."

"One more favor, if you will," Aleja went on. "Could you give me air force transportation, something small like a C-21? I usually fly coach on commercial airlines, but in this case, I think speed is critical. With all that's going on, there could be flight delays."

"Absolutely agree," Kahn said. "Consider it done. Going back to what you said earlier, even you might be a target for the Iranians, so I'll provide Secret Service protection as well."

"I'm okay with my own security detail and camera crew. That's all we can get on a C-21 anyway, and I don't want this to be a production. Something simple and quick, in and out. And hopefully with some direct German security as well. A couple of Marine Hueys to transport us to and from Ramstein would be ideal."

"Sure, whatever you prefer," Kahn exclaimed, clapping in the background. "It is a true pleasure to work with you, Senator. I look forward to much more of this type of collaboration between our parties in the future."

"As do I, Mr. President. In our hearts, we are both committed to the survival of our nation."

"Agreed. See you tomorrow."

Aleja immediately called Henry Little Hawk. "All set," she said.

"Good work, Aleja. I will call General Bascom and make sure he is personally involved in this transport."

CHAPTER 21

THE PRESS CONFERENCE WENT over without a hitch, and then Aleja, Maria, and her ex-SEAL security team and two-man camera crew made their trip to Biosafe in Berlin on board an air force C-21. They were picked up at Ramstein AFB by the two Hueys and flown into Berlin to a park large enough for the choppers to set down. From there, they were driven the two miles to the Biosafe manufacturing compound by a combined team of German Special Forces and Navy SEALs. She had been briefed by Henry Little Hawk on the selection of pilots and crews for both the C-21 and the Hueys. SEAL Team Six, the pride of the navy, had been personally *volunteered* by Admiral Abrams, who was also coordinating with German Special Forces.

When they reached the Biosafe compound, they were met by a swarm of reporters and throngs of self-identified German Iranians carrying signs chastising the Americans for blaming Iran for the anthrax attack. Others carried banners chiding Senator Trujillo for siding with Kahn.

German police were already onsite, but they were far outnumbered, and the German Special Forces commander called in for military backup. He then approached Aleja directly and

said, "Senator, the number of protestors is increasing rapidly. While we can confirm that no arms got through our check-
points into this area, the sheer numbers are not good. If
violence breaks out, there could be deaths. My command sug-
gests you leave at once."

Aleja narrowed her eyes, scanning the crowds, and felt a
shiver of vertigo overtake her, making it clear she was not as
well as she had thought. The everything-was-too-good-to-be-
true impression she had felt in her discussion with President
Kahn two days ago came back to her, and she saw that she had
been taken advantage of.

"We should have known this would happen," Maria said to
her angrily, as the SEALs closed in around them. "They are not
speaking Farsi," one of the SEALs said, using a parabolic microphone that could reach out into the crowds. "In addition
to German, we're hearing English, Russian, Saudi, Turkish, and
Hebrew."

"A clever setup," Aleja responded, taking a deep breath
to clear her head, "but even more reason why we must go in.
Now!"

She spun around and knocked on the front door of the facility. When she identified herself and asked to come in, she
was met by Anton Olderian, who introduced himself as the
president of Biosafe. "This is a very pleasant surprise," he said
to her, peering apprehensively into the crowds, "but I fear it is
not safe for you here at this time. My security chief is telling
me the German command would like you to leave immediately before violence breaks out."

Aleja gave Olderian a cold stare. "We came to make this
a positive experience for both of us. I am going to be much
safer in here than out there," she said. "I would hate to have
to tell the American public that I was turned away from safe

haven by Biosafe. That may not be the kind of press either of us needs right now."

He nodded and showed her and her team inside. She asked the SEAL team and German Special Forces to stay outside to monitor the situation there.

Olderian led them quickly into his office, which had huge windows overlooking the manufacturing floors below. "I am so happy you are recovering, Senator," he said, wiping the sweat from his brow. "We of course want to give the people of your country confidence that we are on schedule with the vaccine."

"Could you then please show us through the plants?" Aleja responded. "I think if we could show the scale of the operation close up, it would calm a lot of jittery nerves in our country. From what I can see from the outside, there are also plenty of jittery nerves in this country."

Olderian hesitated momentarily, then said, "Yes of course. But let me explain in advance that we have recently modified our lines with new technology that allows us to create and package our vaccine much faster. We are currently seeing about a twenty percent increase from our former model. With the higher speed, though, comes higher possibility for contamination. Hence, the whole plant is now totally clean— biosuits only. We cannot not let you onto the floors, but you can film from the corridors."

"Of course," Aleja said. "Let's get to it, then. The sooner we get started, the sooner we can get out of here before anything starts outside."

Olderian introduced them to his six-man security team, who would be leading the tour. Something suddenly didn't seem right to Aleja, not only the size of the team, but the military-style H&K MP7 compact machine guns on their belts.

Olderian went on. "Due to the importance of this operation, we will be passing through many weapons detectors. I'd like to ask you to leave your weapons here in the office."

"No problem," she answered, having anticipated as much, "but your guns don't set them off?" She nodded to the security officers.

"They do facial scans for identification as we go through the various portals. Once they're authenticated, the detectors are programmed to let them pass."

"I see," Aleja answered, seeing no point in carrying the discussion further. She motioned for her four guards to leave their sidearms on Olderian's desk. "My camera crew doesn't carry weapons," she said, "but you're welcome to scan us all if you like." She extended her arms.

"If you don't mind," Olderian said. One of his security team used a portable x-ray scanner on her and her team, then nodded that they were all good to go. "Please follow us."

Aleja and her team moved through a total of three warehouses. As they walked, she carried on a narrative with Olderian while her ex-SEAL camera crew captured everything on tape.

"How much longer before all the shipments will be ready?" she asked Olderian as they moved through the facility.

"With the faster production model here, we'll be done in about two weeks."

They wound through several block-long corridors, passing through entry portals where Olderian and his guards performed facial scans to get them through. On the other sides of the portals, Aleja was amazed to see space-age floors with hundreds of staffers in biosuits working feverishly.

"Very impressive," she said, staring at the highly advanced biosuits and the care with which the workers were handling the products on the lines. "I've heard you are working twenty-four seven?" Aleja asked.

"Yes, we have three full shifts."

"Just for my own curiosity, do those boxes on the conveyor belts contain the actual nasal spray units?"

"Yes," he said, looking more uneasy with each question.

"Could you have your team bring us a couple of those packages?" she said. "It would be great for me to take back a few for some of our leading scientists to test. If I bring them back personally, it would go a long way toward increasing public confidence in your program."

"I am afraid that will not be possible," Olderian said, motioning for his security team to surround them. The six guards drew their MP7s from their belts and pointed them at Aleja and her team. "Please stop filming immediately," one of the guards ordered.

Maria surprised Olderian from his blind side and put him into a choke hold. "I can snap your neck in a second," she said, pointing him at his security detail. "Tell them to put down their weapons."

"You will never get out of here alive," Olderian snarled.

"Neither will you," Maria responded, increasing the pressure on his throat to cut off his air.

"Settle down, everyone," Aleja replied calmly. "We will do as you say. Maria, let him breathe." Then to her camera crew, she said, "Stop filming now."

She stood staring at the security detail as her two cameramen followed her instructions. "All off," they both said, then pulled the triggers of the specially designed dazzler flash guns concealed in their cameras.

The overpowering bursts of light temporarily blinded the Biosafe guards, giving Aleja's ex-SEAL security detail the opening to rush the disabled guards and snatch their machine guns.

"Now let's get the samples," she said to Olderian. She took his arm on the other side of Maria and forced him to lead them onto the production floor. The biosuited workers froze at the sight of them.

"We shouldn't be in here," Olderian said, growing pale.

"Ah," Aleja responded, "so now we're getting somewhere. There must be live anthrax spores in here. Best you hurry then. I have already been vaccinated. But if my daughter is infected, I am going to be very unhappy with you."

"I am not afraid to die for our cause to rid the world of your kind," Olderian said combatively. "And none of my men are afraid to die either. You are not getting any of this vaccine, and you will not leave here alive. Pull the alarm!" he called out to the floor. Sirens immediately went off as one of the workers pulled a red lever at the side of the room.

Maria put Olderian back in a choke hold and forced him in front of her mother, where he was hit by the first volley of gunfire from guards rushing in from the other side of the building. The camera crew fired their dazzlers again, disabling the first batch of newly arrived guards, while Aleja's security detail fired their commandeered machine guns at the clusters of other Biosafe guards arriving from other parts of the complex. At the sound of the gunfire and the effect of the flash lasers, the biosuited workers panicked and ran in all directions, creating enough of a diversion to allow Aleja's team to snatch boxes of vaccine off the conveyor belts. With the samples secured, Aleja and her team followed the workers through an exit on the other side of the floor.

"Get us to the street," Maria said in German to one of the frightened workers.

"Through there," the man replied in German, pointing to door with the sign, "Notausgang (Fire Exit)." But before they could get there, new teams of Biosafe guards converged on them from either side. The dazzler team disabled the group to their left but were wounded by a team on their blind sides. Aleja called for her the rest of her team to rush for cover behind a row of forklifts where they could shoot it out. But with both dazzlers down, it was only a matter of time before they would be outnumbered or run out of ammunition.

"I can get one of the dazzlers," Maria said to her in a shaky voice.

"No!" Aleja said, seeing the dazed look in her daughter's eyes of young soldiers in their first firefight, desperate to take action even if it was not rationale. "I'll go."

"Like hell," Maria mumbled, coming to her feet erratically. "Cover me," she panted to her mother, leaping from behind the forklift and running toward the wounded camera crew.

Aleja jumped after her, tackling her as bullets pounded on all sides of them. In a daze, Maria pushed Aleja away and came to her feet again but was hit in the leg, bringing her down screaming in pain. Aleja turned and took careful aim in the biosafe shooters, her muscle memory turning her into a deadly shot even though she was terrified for her daughter. She brought two of the Biosafe Guards down, giving her SEALs open shots at the others. She crawled to Maria and covered her with her body while her SEALs picked off the remaining guards and seized their weapons.

Aleja called for help to get Maria and the wounded cameramen to their feet, and then they all staggered for the fire exit. Outside, when the huge crowd of protestors saw Aleja and her team emerge, they rushed the German police, but German Special Forces quickly interceded to help the police hold their line. The protestors remained undeterred, however, and hurled rocks and other debris toward Aleja, forcing the SEALs to surround her and her team to give them cover. The two Hueys, which had been hovering overhead, descended onto the street, and the SEALs rushed Aleja and Maria onto the first chopper, and helped the rest of her team into the second. As the Hueys lifted away from the angry protestors, Aleja ripped off her blouse and made a tourniquet to stop the gushing blood from Maria's leg. "I'm okay, Momma," Maria said deliriously, dripping in sweat. "I'm sorry I got shot."

Aleja pulled her daughter tightly into her arms, brushing the sweat-soaked hair away from her eyes. "I am very proud of you," she said, gasping for breath. "Your father would have been proud too. You don't have to be sorry about anything."

The Hueys sped out of the city, escorted by two German Eurofighter Typhoons and two American F-16s. Twenty minutes later, the choppers set down at Ramstein AFB, and Maria was rushed onto their US-bound C-21. A medical team was already on board, waiting for her and the other wounded. As the jet lifted off, Maria lost consciousness. Aleja watched frantically as the medics gave her oxygen and blood. During the long flight back to Dulles, Aleja never let go of Maria's hand, cursing herself for letting her baby come. She prayed that Maria would come out of this alive and fully recovered. This battle had brought out a part of her that she'd done her best to subdue since leaving active duty as a SEAL. Kahn would pay for this. There would be no rest for her until she had unleashed her wrath on him.

CHAPTER 22

PRESIDENT KAHN ACTIVATED HIS secured video-conference bridge and addressed Stanyan, Vanderhurst, Edgewood, Army general Lancaster, and CDC Director Shaw. "I will be holding a larger meeting with the senior members of the Nationalist party to debrief them on the attack on Biosafe earlier today by Senator Trujillo, and aside from having to put together a whole strategy in response, I want to know how she found out about the second Biosafe lines?"

"It didn't come from anyone in my agency," Director Shaw answered. "I have been working alone and will continue to do so. I know I have the highest probability of a leak in my organization because my people are not sworn."

"And nothing from my people," Edgewood said. "My teams are all handpicked by me."

General Lancaster responded, "I am the only one in the army who knows of this particular aspect of the plan."

Kahn nodded and turned his attention to Stanyan and Vanderhurst and waited for their responses.

Stanyan rubbed at his very red eyes and shook his head. "Vanderhurst and I are the only ones who knew about the second Biosafe line in the CCC. Same as the director and the general. You know that we are totally committed to the mission."

"What about McAnter?" Kahn asked. "Is there some way he could have found out?"

Stanyan craned his neck, looking over at Vanderhurst with a grimace. "Yes, I suppose he could if he wanted to, but he's always been a supporter of yours. I don't know why he would go to the effort of doing something like that. Not only would he have had to use Sentinel in a highly secretive manner, but then he'd have to have contacted Senator Trujillo in an equally secretive manner. We've been with him nearly twenty-four hours a day and he just doesn't strike me as the kind to do something like that."

"Is there anything that might have happened recently to motivate him to do all this?" Kahn pressed.

"In our status meeting yesterday, McAnter found the live chips in the system, and I felt I had to explain to him what they were for," Stanyan replied. "He was pretty surprised, but I believe I convinced him that the information was top secret. He knows he's working for the military. What about a sneaky reporter who may have been snooping around Biosafe in Germany?"

"They would have broken the story on the air," Kahn came back testily. "Somebody has to have taken this information directly to Trujillo. Trace your logs to see if McAnter made any calls or sent any messages."

Vanderhurst worked with Sentinel on his tablet. After a few moments, he responded, "The only outside communications Dr. McAnter made in the last two weeks were to his wife. He calls her almost every day, except the last call was the night before the LA attack. After that, just a few text messages while he was at the DWP in LA. Nothing since he got back to Eagle's Cliff."

"That's a little odd, isn't it?"

Vanderhurst nodded.

"Would it have been as easy for him to just ask Sentinel some questions like you just did and get back the answers?"

"Sentinel is certainly capable of doing that," Vanderhurst said. "I thought you understood that before we installed it. Sentinel can answer any question for which it has data. There is plenty of data available now to give away the entire plan."

Kahn narrowed his eyes at Vanderhurst challengingly. "Is there a way you can check if McAnter asked any questions?"

"Already started that query into Sentinel," Vanderhurst said. Several moments later, he added, "Here are Dr. McAnter's queries into the system over the past two weeks." He shared his screen on the conference bridge. "This is just normal work he does to keep Sentinel running."

"Could someone have hacked the system?" Kahn asked.

Stanyan shook his head. "That's the whole purpose of Sentinel, to be sure it can't be hacked. McAnter has built in extensive measures to prevent that."

Kahn got up and started pacing around the room. "Unless he was the one who did the hacking."

Vanderhurst sat forward. "He could have created a secret user ID or back door into the system."

"Which means what?" Kahn said.

Stanyan answered, "It means that McAnter may be able to operate within the system without anyone knowing."

"And how are we going to find out if he has such a little key to the back door?" Kahn responded sarcastically.

"It won't be easy," Vanderhurst said. "And if he does have one, we can't let him anywhere near the system again. But we also can't operate the system in its current state of development without him."

Kahn continued to pace, shaking his head and cursing under his breath. "Then we are just going to have to make sure he's on board with us," he said. "Director Edgewood, why don't you pay a visit to McAnter's family?"

"You sure you want to do that?" Stanyan came in. "If he's innocent, you've just made him into an enemy. A very dangerous one."

Kahn threw up his arms in exasperation. "Let's go over this one more time, dammit. Is there anyone else who could have simply asked Sentinel what the fuck is going on?"

"There are different levels of access to Sentinel," Vanderhurst answered. "Only McAnter, the general, Edgewood, and I have advanced query access."

"In that case," Kahn came in heatedly, "assuming it's not one of the three of you, McAnter could have found out who really organized the LA attack and told the Resistance. Which means we're about one step away from all hell breaking loose." Placing his full attention on Edgewood now, he said, "McAnter's family is your highest priority. If the Resistance is planning to use McAnter to help bring me down, we have to make sure he knows the stakes he's playing for."

CHAPTER 23

BUR WAS IN HIS office waiting to hear from Jenks about his extraction from Eagle's Cliff when Stanyan and Vanderhurst rumbled in.

"We need to talk," Stanyan said, shutting the door behind him.

Bur sat back in his seat, not liking the expression on Stanyan's face.

"Are you aware of Senator Trujillo's little caper yesterday where she killed almost a dozen guards at Biosafe and took some of the vaccine?"

Bur narrowed his eyes, surprised. "It's been all over the news."

Stanyan took a seat across from Bur and rubbed at his forehead with the palm of his hand. "The attack is being blamed on the Iranians, but we know she did it. Do you have any idea why she would take such drastic action?"

"No idea," Bur lied.

"Paulo and I have been wracking our brains about where she might have gotten whatever information motivated her to do this? Did you give her any? The kind that only Sentinel could find?"

Bur kept his eyes directly on Stanyan as he responded, "No, I did not."

"Very interesting. We checked all your outgoing phone and texting logs and found nothing associated with you other than your call to your family last week before you went to LA and a few texts while you were there. But nothing since you got back to Eagle's Cliff. Is that because you have cloaked your calls? And maybe have a secret back door into Sentinel that allows you to do searches anonymously? And maybe you called Senator Trujillo with whatever information you stealthily discovered and hence motivated her to attack Biosafe?"

Bur took in a deep breath, knowing he'd have to do his very best to lie his way out of this. "Sounds pretty cloak-and-dagger. Something like that would take a lot of work. I don't have that kind of time, if you hadn't noticed."

Vanderhurst came in. "I agree; it would be a major undertaking. But then again, Sentinel is a major undertaking, too, and you managed to pull that off."

Stanyan took over again. "What we need to know, Bur, is what else you might know and might therefore have passed on to Senator Trujillo and the Resistance."

"I don't have a secret back door into Sentinel, and I didn't share any information with Senator Trujillo," Bur responded, very worried now that he could keep up the subterfuge. "And just what information would cause her to do such a thing?"

"I want to believe you, Bur, I really do," Stanyan replied, "but the stakes are incredibly high here, and Sentinel is a very powerful tool that knows all. I think we may have not fully comprehended that as we were heads-down building it. But if you're lying to us and you do have a back door, then you are a major risk to us. We need you to tell us what you know, and then we need you to reverse whatever information you might have given to Senator Trujillo. If you're her inside man, then we can use you to our advantage—provided you pledge to fully support us and do exactly what we tell you."

Bur's temper flared. "I have always followed orders, and I will continue to do so."

Stanyan smiled. "Excellent. I guess that settles it, then. But just in case you might change your mind..." He placed his smart tablet on Bur's desktop and brought up the video of Bur's last call with his family before he'd gone to fix the cyber-attack at DWP. Bur's anger peaked as he stared at Jimmy playing with Genny and her new teddy bear. He wanted to lunge for Stanyan's throat, but sucked in his anger, relieved to know that his family was safe with Senator Trujillo.

"You're indeed going to take our orders, Bur," Stanyan went on, listening to Bur's exchange with his wife and children on the tablet. "Then your family can continue to live a happy, healthy life, right where they are. Otherwise, we might have to bring them up here."

Bur gritted his teeth, surprised and disgusted that Stanyan could resort to this kind of tactic after all they'd been through together to get Sentinel up and running. "My wife and kids have nothing to do with any of this. Leave them alone."

"Nothing I'd rather do. Follow our instructions precisely, and they'll be just fine."

Bur's anger crested again as he watched Jimmy tickle his little sister under her chin and make her giggle. "So what happened to the utopia we were going to build, General?" he said.

"It is still going to happen, Bur. Have faith. We only take these drastic measures to ensure your vision is carried out."

Bur paced back and forth in front of Stanyan's tablet, which continued to play the video call and now showed Carmen putting Genny to bed. The thick auburn braid of his wife's long hair hung innocently over his daughter's cheek, making Bur squirm as Stanyan watched her. Bur felt himself getting dizzy as he thought through what could have happened if he had not contacted Senator Trujillo when he did.

"I need your pledge that you'll do as we tell you," Stanyan said.

Bur nodded. "I will do as you tell me."

Stanyan motioned for Bur to follow him to the control center floor. "We are going to do the microchip implant distribution tomorrow. All schedules must be maintained more than ever now after what happened yesterday at Biosafe. You need to work with Paulo to get the master distribution list out ASAP. I hope I don't have to ever remind you again what will happen if you fuck around with us."

"I got the message," Bur responded. He turned to Vanderhurst and said, "If you can send me your master list, I'll verify it against the CNID database and make any necessary changes. Then I'll work with Sentinel to build the routing algorithm that will direct people to the least busy distribution center."

Vanderhurst sat down at his own console seat next to Bur's and passed over the information. He waited for a few minutes for Bur to confirm he had what he needed, then went back to his own work. Just as soon as Bur could see that Vanderhurst was fixed on his own screen, he opened a small window on his monitor and invoked AIPOTU. *Connect me with Jenks.* A few seconds later, Jenks sent back a text. *Good to hear from you. Much going on. Senator Trujillo has the samples from Biosafe, and we're ready to go public but need you to provide the details of how you got the information from Sen. Time for you to get out.*

Bur was elated to hear the news but contained his sigh of relief. *Stanyan suspects I'm involved,* he typed back, then suddenly minimized the window as Vanderhurst looked over from his own monitor to check on him. Bur quickly went back to working on a routing algorithm. Vanderhurst seemed satisfied and went back to his own work.

It was only a matter of time, Jenks typed as Bur expanded the text window on his screen again. *We're ready to extract you. Patching in Henry, who's at Vandenburg.*

Several minutes passed before Bur got a text message back. *Hello, Doctor*, Little Hawk wrote. *I can be at Eagle's Cliff in twenty minutes by chopper. Are you able to get out of the complex, and is there a place we can pick you up?*

Yes, there's a helipad on top of the three-story dorm.

Let me know when you're on the pad. We'll take off now and circle till you call or text.

Bur quickly closed the window and returned to his work for a few moments, finishing up routing routine for the distribution, but making one last change before he saved the program. He had to have a backup plan in case this all went wrong. "Ready to go," he said to Vanderhurst. "If we start now, we should be done by tonight."

Vanderhurst nodded, briefly making eye contact.

"I need a cigarette," Bur responded. "Okay if I go up to the Stream?"

Vanderhurst called over to Stanyan, "He wants to have a cigarette."

Bur cut in. "Come on, what am I gonna do, jump?"

Stanyan grunted and nodded. "Five minutes, Doctor; then we need to see where we are with your new algorithm." Turning back to Vanderhurst, Stanyan said, "Why don't you go with him? Maybe you guys can become friends after all." He reached out his pistol to Vanderhurst.

"I don't need that," Vanderhurst said, grinning and pushing the gun away. "I was a field agent before I was transferred to IT. Too much excessive force." He laughed.

Bur did a facial scan on the infrared reader, the door opened, and he scrambled up the three flights to the top of the building. Authenticating once again at the outside door, he rushed into the open air of the bridge and lit up a cigarette.

Vanderhurst, on his tail, lit up as well. "Looks like you're not quite as smart as you thought you were, Doctor."

"Appears that way." Bur took a big drag. The nicotine rush made his mind keener. He started walking along the twelve-foot-wide corridor called the Stream, the main thoroughfare between work and the dormitory. Vanderhurst walked with him. Most staffers were having dinner in the cafeteria at this time of day, so the Stream was empty.

"You're going to be king of the hill on the project," Bur remarked as they walked, unable to contain his anger at Vanderhurst's betrayal, "but I doubt you'll be up to the task without me in command."

"Very funny, Doctor. I didn't see you laughing when Stanyan said he would bring your wife up here. She is very beautiful. If anything should happen to you, I would indeed be the king of the hill, and I could have all your privileges."

Bur hit him before he could stop himself. He caught the taller man on the ear with a wild left hook that didn't have much behind it.

"You son of a bitch!" Vanderhurst yelled. "I've been waiting for that." He hit Bur on the jaw with a vicious punch that sent him flying into the inner wall of the complex. Bur's head rebounded off the concrete and his eyes blurred. Shaking his head, he tried to duck as Vanderhurst swung again. He was too late. The larger man's fist collided with his nose. Blood gushed.

Bur mustered all his strength to shove Vanderhurst away, sucking in air through his mouth. Vanderhurst slipped out of his grasp and charged, connecting with his ribs. Vanderhurst smiled. "Now I'm really going to fuck you up."

He swung again, but Bur deflected the blow, surprising him, and counterpunched like he had in the many fights he'd had in high school protecting Carmen or his family of nerds. Aiming for Vanderhurst's own ribs, his strike was on the money this time, and he doubled Vanderhurst over. He tried for a couple of head shots, but Vanderhurst easily deflected them and brought Bur down roughly on the concrete floor of the Stream. Cracking the back of his head again, Bur saw stars, and for a moment flashed back to watching Carmen put Genevieve to bed. He rolled over with a growl and caught Vanderhurst on the tip of the chin with his elbow, then wobbled to his feet so he could throw a better punch. But Vanderhurst took his legs out from under him with a fancy kick, bringing him into the hard cement yet again. Bur struck out with his own legs and brought Vanderhurst down on top him, face-to-face. He wrapped his powerful arms around the bigger man and then smashed his forehead into Vanderhurst's face. A shower of blood covered them both as he struck again and again. Vanderhurst tried to get his arms free from Bur's iron grasp, but Bur held on. One by one, Bur's blows took their toll. Vanderhurst choked for breath through Bur's bear hug.

"Stop!" Vanderhurst wheezed.

Bur wasn't sure he was hearing right and pulled his arms in tighter around Vanderhurst's body.

"Stop!" Vanderhurst cried again.

Bur's body fought with his mind to keep going, but his mind finally won out. Whatever strength it would take to finish off Vanderhurst at this point was all he had left to escape. He let up his hold and secured Vanderhurst's hands behind his back with his own belt. Vanderhurst rolled away from him, choking on the blood flowing from his mouth. Bur dragged himself to his feet and had the momentary impulse to kick Vanderhurst's head to finish him off, but he didn't. He pulled out his phone and signed into AIPOTU.

"Lock the complex down, take out the lights, and start the sprinklers," he said, too wound up to text. He knew that every system in the facility was under Sentinel's control since the downloads.

"Affirmative," Sentinel replied.

Bur watched the lights go out and heard the cries of distress below as the sprinklers turned on. He staggered along the walkway toward the dormitory, looking for the stairs up to the helipad. With all inside and outside lights now cut, he used his cell phone light to find his way. Struggling up the two flights of stairs to the helipad, he stepped over the safety railing and breathed in the bitter sea breeze coming up from the pounding surf on the cliffs below. Staring into the moonless sky, he heard the chatter of a helicopter in the distance. He dialed Henry. "I am on the helipad," he said. "Look for my light in the dark."

He brushed the blood from his eyes and pictured his family in his mind one last time, praying he would be with them again soon. Waving his phone light in the dark, he watched the chopper bank in toward him, turning on its landing lights. He hurried to meet it and was pulled inside by the strong arms of Henry Little Hawk.

CHAPTER 24

STANYAN RECOILED AS THE lights and power abruptly went out across the control center. What the hell was this? He came to his feet and turned on his cell phone light to see, the same as everyone else in the room. No one seemed sure what to do, and everyone looked to him for guidance. He was about to tell them to stay put, because the backup generators would kick on in less than a minute, but then the fire alarms went off and the sprinklers came on.

People broke and scurried for the exits. He got up and splashed through water on the floor with them, concerned about what all this was going to do to his computer systems. He tried to calm his staff as people crammed into the halls and stairwells on their way down to ground level. The blaring of the alarms, the rain from the sprinklers, and the dancing beams of the cell phone lights created a surreal milieu. Several people slipped in the water, and he rushed to help them up before they were trampled. When he finally reached ground level, the water was even deeper. He stomped outside along with the rest of his staff. He was about to head toward the road when he heard a chopper touching down on the helipad above them. The landing light of the chopper clearly framed McAnter as he was lifted in. Enraged, Stanyan waded back inside against the outcoming traffic. He hurried toward the landing pad three flights above. Pushing open the security door, he emerged into the evening blackness and ran for the helipad. Focusing on the taillight of the chopper as it sped away, he tripped and fell over Vanderhurst on the floor of the Stream.

"What the fuck?" he cried, freeing Vanderhurst's wrists from behind his back. "How did you let him get away from you?"

Vanderhurst shook his head, wiping the blood from his face. "He hit me by surprise, then got picked up by a Huey."

"I can see that, goddammit!" Stanyan hollered. "I sent you up here with him to make sure he didn't try anything, and now he's gone!" He pulled Vanderhurst to his feet and shoved him toward the stairway. "Get the fucking sprinklers turned off and the lights back on!"

In no mood for any other surprises, he pulled out his cell phone and called Edgewood. "Do you have McAnter's wife yet?"

"No," Edgewood replied. "When we got to her flat in San Francisco, she was gone. We checked with her neighbors, and one of them said he saw a black SUV take them away very late last night. The neighbor couldn't identify who took them, except that a woman was leading the group."

"Senator Trujillo, of course!" Stanyan screamed. "She must have picked up McAnter's family right before she left for Germany."

"My conclusion as well. I used Sentinel to check Mrs. McAnter's phone and video records, but there's nothing there."

"Clearly cloaked by McAnter. What else can you do to find her?"

"Assuming it was the senator who picked her up, she would have put Mrs. McAnter somewhere she feels is safe. That could be almost anywhere in California, or she could have brought her to Washington. But since this trip had to be put together very quickly, and she led it personally, I'm betting she was using people very close to her. I think she'd stay in an area where she wouldn't draw undue attention."

"And?" Stanyan said.

"I had my teams check local airports close to her, since she certainly didn't have time to drive back and forth between LA and San Francisco. My men discovered that a private plane owned by a close colleague of Senator Trujillo's left the Santa Monica Municipal Airport at 12:17 a.m. the day before Senator Trujillo departed for Washington for her press conference with President Kahn. That plane retuned to SMO at 7:04 a.m. that same day. Because of this unusual flight plan, we believe there is a good chance that Senator Trujillo and the McAnters were on it, and that the McAnters are currently somewhere in Santa Monica or Venice. Therefore, we are working with our internal drone team to search for Mrs. McAnter's and her kids' voiceprints with both laser and parabolic microphones. We got their voiceprints from McAnter's last call with them before he cloaked them."

"I have those prints too," Stanyan replied, beginning to like what he was hearing. "And those audio drones aren't scheduled to be connected to Sentinel until all the video cameras are finished."

"Precisely," Edgewood responded. "There is no way for them to be cloaked by whatever McAnter did to Sentinel. We have ten drones up, focusing on ten square miles, one square mile each. With such limited scanning orbits, these new microphones can pick up every human voice in their areas and check it against the McAnters' voiceprints."

"Excellent," Stanyan replied. "Let me know the minute you find her."

CHAPTER 25

EDGEWOOD HAD NOT BOTHERED to get into the non-technological details of this mission with Stanyan, since this was not the general's area of expertise. What Edgewood had left out was his hypothesis that Senator Trujillo would be expecting the McAnters to be found and had chosen her own turf in case it came to a fight. Mrs. McAnter and her kids would no doubt be surrounded by former SEALS and other professionals, well armed and well trained. This was not going to be a clandestine operation; it was going to be a full-out battle. He had done clandestine removals all around the world in more hostile environments than this. His team was every bit as well trained as whatever they were going to encounter. The difference would be which team was more ruthless. His advantage was that he and his men hated the Resistance more than any of the corrupt dictators they had brought down around the world in the name of freedom. His teams would have no concern whatsoever for collateral damage. As a matter of fact, the more the better.

He and his San Francisco team met the LA team at the south city municipal parking lot near Venice Pier. In addition to his field teams, his recon team was set up in a large van with a dish on top. "What do we know?" he asked his recon lead.

"We got a hit on McAnter's boy about two hours ago," the recon lead said. "The kid's a big talker. His mother was able to get a word in now and then to confirm her voice print as well. They're in an apartment above the Black Dragon Tattoo Parlor on Windward, about a block east of Ocean Front Walk. Very heavy foot traffic in that area, and Windward is not a through street. No chance of getting them out by car. There are two apartments above the parlor. The one they have the McAnters in is furthest from the street, with a fire escape to a small alley behind. The main entrance is from a door to one side of the parlor. Two guards in front, two in back. The parlor is busy with five tattoo artists and lots of people waiting at this time of night. Pretty sure several of the waiting customers are additional security. There are walking guards on either side of the street, both male and female. We spotted six, but there could be more. One team of two in a car directly across from the street. The car never moves, but we've seen teams rotating in and out. All of their teams are using walkie-talkies, apparently to prevent detection by our satellites, but the drones are capturing everything they say, so we'll know immediately if we've been detected or they are moving the McAnters."

The LA field team lead spoke next. "Our best option is to create a diversion in the streets to give us cover to enter from both the front and the alley in the back," he said. "The alley comes out on a small public parking lot. We will have teams there for cover, but the diversion will block all traffic in the area, so we'll need to transport the McAnters on foot to the beach to get picked up by our chopper. That's almost half a mile in the middle of a full-scale panic. We run the risk that we won't get them out alive."

"They're no good to us dead," Edgewood responded curtly. "We get them out at any cost."

His men all nodded and then proceeded toward the tattoo parlor. His twenty-man team each carried two smoke bombs in backpacks and wore casual clothing that helped them fit into the local crowds. As midnight approached, the streets were jammed with crowds on their way to bars and restaurants. Edgewood stationed two-man teams in a perimeter at the intersections of Ocean Walk and Winward, Winward and Speedway, Speedway and Seventeenth Street, then Seventeenth and Winward. He kept two teams close to him, although they did not walk together. As he passed the parlor for his first recon, two men eyed him carefully. He responded coolly, putting in his earbuds. Two others were stationed directly across the street in a car, keeping a vigilant eye on the parlor and the heavy foot traffic in front of it. Edgewood picked up no other obvious guards in the area but knew that there would be rovers on patrol. He gave the order over his cell phone for his teams on the perimeter to set off their smoke bombs. And then all hell broke loose.

Screams filled the air as the crowds broke and ran. He and his men put on their gas masks and set off a smoke bomb in front of the parked car. Then they threw another on the steps to the apartments above the parlor. The Resistance guards near the steps and in the parked car quickly produced handguns and opened fire, pinning them in a crossfire and cutting down two of his four-man squad. Edgewood called for backup but heard heavy gunfire around the area as the Resistance engaged with his teams.

Exhilarated by the gunfire, Edgewood used the stampeding crowds to his advantage, taking a shot through them to bring down one of the parlor guards, then pushed a throng of young people into the other guard, occupying his attention long enough to bring him down. He quickly looked back for his other two men, but they were fighting for their lives as more heavily armed Resistance appeared out of nowhere.

Rushing into the smoke-filled parlor, he pulled off half a dozen quick shots to bring down the armed Resistance who confronted him. Kicking in the door that led to the apartments, he raced up the stairs, but immediately drew fire from the two Resistance guards stationed at the door of the rear apartment. Retreating into the stairwell, he rolled a smoke bomb down the hall, waited for it to go off, then peppered the guards with bullets. Groans followed, but there was no return fire. He snapped in a new clip of ammo and proceeded carefully. He came upon the dead guards in front of the door where he assumed Mrs. McAnter and her children must be.

CHAPTER 26

CARMEN MCANTER SHUDDERED AT the knock at her door. She'd heard shots outside and could smell a foul smoke coming under the door. "Mrs. McAnter, I'm from the Resistance," she heard a man call. "Senator Trujillo sent me to get you out of here. Please open the door. We must move right now."

"Where are Tommy and Roberto?" she called back.

The door shuddered as someone kicked it from the other side. The dead bolt held.

"Shark attack!" Carmen called out to her children, turning off the lights and racing for her broom. She listened in the dark as Jimmy and Genevieve scrambled for their weapons and came to stand bravely at her side. "To the back," she whispered.

They moved rapidly through the darkness, just like they had practiced several times earlier in the day with their eyes closed. But before they reached the back door, there was a crash from the front one. A light beam captured her. "Freeze, Mrs. McAnter."

The intruder didn't see Jimmy and Genevieve coming in silently from his sides. Genevieve sprayed him in the face with the wasp killer, and Jimmy hit him below his belt with his brass candlestick, eliciting a yelp, then a curse. Carmen wasted no time. She attacked with her broom, going for his eyes, but hit his cheek instead, provoking another cry.

Abandoning the idea of staying behind to fight while her kids escaped, she jabbed the man's chest and screamed at the kids, "Hit him in the legs! Get him down."

Jimmy bashed away with his heavy candlestick. With a wild backhand, the intruder sent the boy flying across the room. Genevieve leaped on the man's back and got her short arms around his neck while Carmen charged, using her broom to trip him. Getting him down on the floor, she pummeled him with her fists as hard as she could, trying to find his nose to break it, like Bur had shown her.

The man suddenly erupted from the floor, knocking her off him, and threw Genevieve to the side. The little girl hit the floor and didn't move. Carmen screamed, coming at the attacker with renewed energy. Jimmy, too, came back, charging the man's legs. "I'll get you for hurting my sister!" he cried.

The man picked up Jimmy by the throat and held him in front of him as a shield. "Stop now!" he said.

Carmen heard Jimmy gasping for air as he flailed. His arms were too short to punch the man. She looked around for another weapon, but could see nothing but Genevieve's motionless body, the sight of which enraged her.

She dove for the man's legs, trying to tackle him. He grabbed her by her long braid and pulled her to her feet, putting his knee into her spine, bending her over backward so he could see into her eyes. "Stop this or I will break you in half."

She screamed as he bent her over further, feeling that her backbone could indeed snap. "Stop."

He released the tension, but kept hold of her hair, preventing her from moving her head to either side. "Tell your brats to do as I say," he whispered into her ear. "Their backs break a lot easier than yours, but it won't kill them—right away."

Her legs were numb from what he'd done to her and she could hear Jimmy choking. "Okay," she said.

He gave her some slack and shoved her toward Genevieve, still holding her by the hair. She bent down and picked up her little girl. Thank God, Genny was still breathing. Cradling her in her arms, she spoke to the intruder through the blackness in front of her. "Let my boy go."

The man shifted Jimmy under his arm like a football and headed for the fire escape, pushing Carmen in front of him by her hair. She feigned a limp to slow him down, but he didn't buy it and forced her to move faster. She looked for help, but the smoke was far too thick, and she choked uncontrollably, as did her children. The attacker forced them into the stair-well, where they were met by two other men. The men took her kids while Edgewood held her by the braid, forcing her down the stairs and into the alley. She tried to keep track of her children but couldn't see through the smoke. She trudged through the alley and emerged into streets bursting with pan-icking men and women. Police sirens came from all directions, and floodlights from police choppers searched for shooters in the streets. Carmen tripped over lifeless or screaming bod-ies until she felt sand under her feet and heard more chop-pers. As she looked around frantically for her kids, the sky lit up with an explosion, and a police chopper crashed into the sand in front of them. Another chopper with no identification sat down immediately thereafter, and she was heaved into it. To her great relief, the children were carried in right after her. She pulled them onto her lap, staring defiantly at the men who closed in around them.

"Settle down, Mrs. McAnter," the man who had hurt them said. "It will do no good to fight."

The chopper lifted off toward the ocean, in the opposite direction of the pandemonium below. She stared around her, seeing no way out, and feared for what might yet be coming for her and her children, and for her husband.

CHAPTER 27

BUR SAT NEXT TO Henry Little Hawk in the chopper as it flew back to Vandenburg. There, after his bloody nose and head wounds from his fight with Vanderhurst had been tended to by an air force doctor, he and Senator Little Hawk were transferred to a C-20 for Washington DC. As he began giving Henry and the air force commander on board a debriefing, he got a call from his wife.

"Let me take this," he said, his mind racing with the ramifications. He got up and went to the back of the plane where he could talk to her in private.

"Carmen?" He was not sure it was her because of the loud noise in the background.

Edgewood's swollen face appeared on his phone. Bur shook his head, unable to comprehend what was happening.

"Surprised to see me?" Edgewood said. "Look who I've found."

Carmen came on his screen, her eyes swollen and her face bloody.

Edgewood laughed at Bur's reaction. "I can tell you that Stanyan and Vanderhurst are very angry with you right now, but I'm actually feeling quite good. Knowing that your wife and kids will be at Eagle's Cliff by daybreak makes me some-what of a hero in their eyes. So much so that the general has given her to me for safekeeping."

Bur trembled with revulsion and anger. "I'll kill you if you lay a hand on her."

Edgewood laughed again. "Now, now, settle down, we have much to discuss. But first, why don't you ask her how she is?"

"Bur?" Carmen muttered, turning her head in the direction of his voice but seeming unable to clearly see him. "Please help us. The kids are both hurt."

Bur froze at the sound of her voice and the vacancy of her stare.

"Ah, so I finally got your attention," Edgewood came back in.

Carmen spoke again desperately. "Bur, they've broken Jimmy's arm. Genevieve's in shock; she may have a concus-sion. He did something to my back, and I can't feel my legs... help us, please!"

"Leave them alone!" Bur growled, trying to keep his voice down so Henry and the general didn't hear him.

Stanyan came onto his screen in a split window next to Edgewood's. "We know that Senator Trujillo is back from Germany. We know that she and Senator Little Hawk are plan-ning to talk to Congress tomorrow in a special session, which will be called now that you are safely on your way there. The timing works out perfectly, since your words will determine whether Congress believes what the senators have to say. Now here's what we want you to do. Your family's very lives depend on it."

Bur listened in silence to Stanyan's demands while Edgewood zoomed Carmen's phone around the cockpit of the chopper, focusing on his crying children, both huddled on his wife's lap.

Stanyan came back on screen. "Now if you cooperate fully, so that we never have to worry about you again, we'll let you stay with your family when you get back here. But if you don't cooperate fully, your wife goes to Edgewood for safekeeping. Not sure what we'll do with your kids. I'm sure he'll think of something, though."

Bur's mind whirled and collided with his emotions as Edgewood put his fingers onto Carmen's puffy eyes, making her scream.

"You follow my orders to the letter," Stanyan said, "or she will scream many more times."

Bur stared at Edgewood, who held Carmen's head with his thumbs positioned directly over her eyes.

"I swear, Stanyan..." Bur growled.

"The angry doctor making empty threats?" Stanyan said. "Now go back to what you were doing, and tell them your wife was rescued by the police after a harrowing confrontation with her kidnappers. Convince them that you are confident they will hold her in safekeeping until you can come for her."

Bur stared at Carmen as she reached out to him, shaking. Then her screen went blank.

Bur collapsed against the window of the plane, unable to stop trembling.

"Doctor, you okay?" Henry Little Hawk said, coming back to check on him.

Bur fought to regain his composure. This had to go right. "My wife and children were taken from Senator Trujillo's safe house, but they've been rescued by the police and are safe. Give me a minute. I just need to gather myself."

"I am so sorry," Henry said putting his hand on Bur's shoulder. "Take all the time you need. At least she's safe."

Bur nodded and said, "I love my family more than anything."

CHAPTER 28

ALEJA AND GENERAL BASCOM arrived by jet cop-
ter on the helipad behind Fort McNair, home of the Military
District of Washington and the Joint Force Headquarters of
US Northern Command. In addition to being the military arm
responsible for homeland defense, Fort McNair was also the
congressional bunker in times of emergency. Since the anthrax smoke bomb attack in Venice last night, Congress and
the president were in lockdown there. A ten-man squad of
Air Force Special Ops commandos hurried them into the command center through a gauntlet of army soldiers. More soldiers patrolled the entire area. Air force jets crisscrossed the
skies overhead.

Aleja was not sure what to expect in light of the second
anthrax attack. Prior to that, she and Henry Little Hawk had
used all their influence to call this special session of Congress,
which they had defined as "of utmost urgency to the safety
of the country." Now, however, under this high-alert situation,
she was not sure if Kahn would even let them talk. No matter what, as members of Congress, they were required to be
there, and she was officially reporting in.

She took in a deep breath and tried to control her emotions as she and General Bascom entered the large underground bunker, set up like the congressional chamber with enough seats for all members and adjacent living quarters for an extended stay if necessary. They remained firmly in the middle of their commando escort, standing just below the speaker's podium, which brought expressions of shock and concern to the faces of the assembled members of Congress.

The Speaker of the House pounded for quiet and introduced the president. Kahn took the podium, staring at Aleja and the general with a perplexed scowl. "We have much to deal with here today, having been attacked again by Iran, and we are indeed on high alert, but I am confounded as to why the senator and general feel the need for their own private guard and why they are not taking a seat?" His attention was drawn away from Aleja and the general by the arrival of Henry Little Hawk and Bur McAnter, who approached the podium from another entrance.

"Ae you okay?" Aleja said to Bur, interrupting the president. She approached Bur and inspected the bruises on his face with concern. The Congress stirred with interest.

"I'm fine, Senator."

"I am sorry that your wife and family have gone through such an ordeal," Aleja went on, keeping her voice low so as not to be overheard. "We had no idea the Nationalists would execute another anthrax attack to cover their attempted kidnapping of your family. But now they're safe. Henry let me know that your wife called you. As soon as we are finished here, we'll fly you directly back to LA to pick them up."

"Let's get on with it," Bur responded glumly. "I'd like to see them as soon as possible."

Aleja turned back to face the president. "We have a guard and have not taken our seats because we are here to provide evidence that you are behind these attacks, not the Iranians. Dr. McAnter, working with Sentinel, has irrefutable proof."

The Congress erupted in shouts and accusations.

"And we have also just obtained proof that you are planning a mass genocide in our country, which appears to be the basis of the LA attacks." She talked over the resulting pandemonium. "I believe the best way to present this evidence is to have Dr. McAnter go over his reports from Sentinel about the details of the LA attack, the planting of anthrax canisters by former members of the CIA, at your direction, and a nefarious scheme to use the anthrax vaccine distribution as a way of killing off your enemies and people of color in our nation." She held out two small boxes. "These are samples of the poison anthrax vaccine that is currently being developed by Biosafe. We also have videos of the deadly production facilities and additional samples in chain-of-custody with both the air force and navy. Finally, we know that you are working with the Russians, Saudis, Turks, and Israelis to create a new world order free of inferior races, however it is that you define 'inferior.'"

The chamber reverberated, rousing General Bascom to order his commandos to tighten in around the senator.

Bur McAnter stepped up to the microphone, next to President Kahn, bringing the chamber to silence. "I am here today to confess to you that I have been involved in a plot by the Resistance, aided by the air force and navy, to take over the country," he said in a gravelly voice.

Aleja snapped her head around, not believing what she had just heard.

Bur went on, "I have been pretending to go along with them, which included my coming here today, in order to find out as much as I could about their plans, so I could report to you. I have found out that Senators Trujillo and Little Hawk,

along with General Bascom and Admiral Abrams, have been
working with a secret coalition of Iranians and Mexicans to
overthrow the US democratic government and replace it with
socialism. It is interesting that they are accusing President
Kahn of doing exactly what they are doing, but with different
actors. The supposed evidence they have brought here today,
portrayed to be a vaccine from Biosafe laced with anthrax,
was developed in Iran's advanced bioterrorism operation in
Tehran. Senator Trujillo went through a deadly staged attack
on Biosafe two days ago, in which several hundred Iranian Al-
Qaeda provided a diversion for her to go into the labs to sabotage the vaccine operation and kill the director and his key
staff. Unfortunately for her, her daughter was hit in one of the
gun battles, forcing her and her team to withdraw before they
could destroy the vaccine production altogether. Her cunning
plan failed when she underestimated my loyalty to my country and President Kahn. Trujillo and Little Hawk assumed that
I would provide fabricated evidence today with which they
could arrest President Kahn. They were dead wrong."

Aleja looked at McAnter in shock as the chamber shook
with shouts and threats from both sides of the aisle. Several
Nationalist congressmen tried to rush the podium but were
pushed back by the commandos. She called out to McAnter
over the din. He would not make eye contact with her, but
rather turned his attention to President Kahn, who was taking
back the microphone.

Kahn called for quiet and faced Aleja and Henry. "I knew
your views were to the left, but I didn't think you'd betray your
country and our democracy, let alone knowingly kill our own
citizens in order to blame it on me."

"Hang her!" came from the Nationalist side of the chamber. Several fights broke out but ended abruptly as a flood of
soldiers swept in from separate doors to restore order.

"This is insanity!" Aleja cried as the soldiers surrounded and handcuffed her and Henry.

The din in the room prevented her from speaking further.

President Kahn motioned for silence. "Based upon this plot to overthrow the government, I am declaring an immediate state of emergency. Curfews will be imposed. The Resistance will be dealt with swiftly and harshly. What we must do now is to ensure that we are prepared for whatever attack is coming, and to arrest anyone we believe may be involved. We have intercepted communications that another, much larger anthrax attack is imminent, and therefore we must take drastic actions. To that end, I have asked for and received confirmation from Biosafe that they will be shipping the vaccines within the next seventy-two hours. Further, in preparation for the vaccine distribution, we will begin the distribution of the microchip implants today. We will announce the locations of distribution centers over our protected network in the next few hours. Citizens without chips will not be able to receive the anthrax vaccine. We must maintain careful control of this life-saving gift and make sure every person in the country has it. We obviously want to guarantee that if anyone is missed in the first distribution, we can immediately get to them in a second distribution."

Aleja's head spun as she and Henry were led through the main aisle of the chamber, threatened and cursed with every step. She tried to make eye contact with McAnter again, but he would not return her gaze.

CHAPTER 29

TEN HOURS LATER, BUR looked below him as the army chopper landed at Eagle's Cliff on the same helipad he had left from the day before. He tried not to think about what he had done in Washington, but the memory of Senator Trujillo's eyes burning into him would not go away. He longed to tell her why he had lied, but knew he might not ever get that opportunity.

Stanyan, Vanderhurst, and Edgewood waited for him on the helipad and stared him down as he got off the chopper. Nothing would have pleased him more than to go after Edgewood right now for what he had done to his wife and children. But he had to keep his anger under control if he was to get his family to safety and prevent Kahn from committing the worst crime in history.

"We are so happy to have you back," Stanyan said sarcastically. "Exceptional job with Congress. President Kahn is elated with your performance and eager to have you back in the saddle. I trust you have lost your urge to wander?"

"Cut the crap," Bur snapped back. "I want to see my family."

"First things first," Stanyan said. "It seems that you have some sort of secret back door to Sentinel that you used to create the reports that Senator Trujillo referred to yesterday. You know everything, don't you, Bur?"

Bur nodded, not breaking eye contact with Stanyan. "I know."

"Our problem is, we are going to need your help now that we are expediting the distribution of the anthrax vaccines. We need you to give us this secret access and ensure that you won't use it again."

Bur had expected this to happen. "I have built the back door into the Sentinel master with a dead man's key that I must disable every twenty-four hours, or it will shut the system down."

Vanderhurst pursed his lips. "I'm almost tempted to see if that's really true, but if it is, you'll need to pass us access to that as well."

"That can't be done," Bur responded. "The disable command is activated from my facial and iris scans. That command filters through the entire authentication process. I cannot provide that access to anyone."

Stanyan and Vanderhurst stared at him. "So that means it's going to shut down in four hours?" he said, looking up at the Control Center clock.

"Yes, that's correct."

"I guess we'll have to call your bluff on that one," Vanderhurst said. "But let's just hypothesize it does what you say, that would mean that if you were to die and never check in again, the system would never work again."

Bur nodded. "That is correct."

"That's just going to have to be fixed, then."

Bur smiled. "That would take days to modify, not hours."

"We'll see how a little more pressure on your family affects the timeline," Edgewood replied. "It seems you were pretty fast to give away your fellow conspirators once we let you know we had your family."

Bur shook his head again, trying to stay calm. "That would require a complete rewrite of the Sentinel master," he responded. "Harming my family isn't going to get that done any faster. So you have to decide whether you want me to rewrite the master or help with the anthrax vaccine distribution."

Stanyan rubbed his hands together and said, "Kahn will not tolerate any changes to the anthrax distribution, so we'll have to go along with you for now. Just don't forget that you won't get any second chances. Next time, Edgewood will make a statement with your family that should cement your hearing."

"I want no more harm to come to my family. May I see them now?"

Vanderhurst looked to Stanyan, who shrugged as if he had no objection. "I can hardly wait to what happens in four hours," Edgewood said. "It seems we have a little time to kill, so I'll show you what your first fuck-up caused."

He led Bur through the maze of corridors to the suite that Bur had occupied for months. Two guards stood at the door.

"Let him in," Edgewood said.

Bur gasped at the sight of Carmen, who sat on his couch with his kids on either side of her. When they saw him, the both shouted with joy and raced to greet him. Bur caught them in his arms and hugged them tearfully, filling with rage as he saw Jimmy's arm in a cast and Genevieve's head bandaged. Carmen reached out for him but couldn't get up. He rushed to her and pulled her gently into his arms. "I'm so sorry," he said into her ear. "Everything's going to be okay."

"Doctor says the feeling will come back into her legs in a couple of days," Edgewood said matter-of-factly. "I guess she took a bad fall. You'll have plenty of time for catching up later; we have business to attend to."

Bur pulled away from his family and faced Edgewood. The big man's eyes danced between Bur and his wife. It was all Bur could do to keep from going for his throat, but he gave his family a final hug and followed him back to the Control Center.

CHAPTER 30

BUR SAT AT HIS workstation across from Stanyan and Vanderhurst, waiting for the large digital clock on the front wall to flash 12:00. When the number changed, nothing happened, bringing Vanderhurst and Stanyan to their feet with glee. "So more bullshit," Vanderhurst said. "Seems we can't believe anything you say."

Bur nodded up at the digital clock. "There is a two-minute buffer built in, just in case I may be slightly delayed."

Both men laughed. "Gotta hand it to you, Doctor," Stanyan said, "you're just full of stories."

"Five, four three, two, one," Bur said, then all the monitors in the center went down and the lights went out. The usual hustle and bustle of the center ceased, and the staff became deathly silent, looking to the ceiling as if expecting the fire sprinklers to go off again.

"Just so you remember," Bur said, "Sentinel now runs all the power grids in the country. You've just turned the nation dark."

Stanyan stormed around the desk to Bur and slammed his fist down. "Get it back up again, goddammit! Now!"

Bur smiled into the glow of Stanyan's cell phone light. "That will require you to manually turn on the backup generators so we can get power back and restore Sentinel from backup."

"Goddammit it, McAnter!" Stanyan screamed and turned to give the orders.

Bur watched with his arms crossed over his chest as the lights came back on and the restore from backup began. He waited patiently until the Sentinel master came up on his and Jenks's workstations, although no one here knew that but him. Stanyan and Vanderhurst hovered over his shoulder, watching.

"Get the rest of it turned on," Stanyan growled.

Bur leaned toward his camera for a facial scan. He prayed Jenks was doing the same. They didn't have to authenticate at the same moment, just within two minutes of each other, as they had always done when bringing up Athena together. Bur let out a sigh of relief as the rest of the computer center came alive and Sentinel resumed normal operations. Jenks had come through.

"You had this all planned out, didn't you?" Stanyan said, glaring at Bur.

Bur nodded. "Yes, I built Sentinel on a number of canons. This authentication canon overrides everything."

"I am going to leave it up to President Kahn to decide next steps," Stanyan responded. "Somehow, some way, I know there's a way for you to fix this. We just need to find out what that is, and President Kahn is a master of that."

CHAPTER 31

JENKS SAT WITH MADELENA in the data center of Crazy Horse University, watching Wolfe News, the only station broadcasting since the state of emergency. All email, chat, and social communities, including Twitter and Facebook, had been cut off. President Kahn was on camera, describing the curfew rules, including no assembly.

"We have learned of yet another anthrax attack in the works by the Iranians and Mexicans now that their inside conspirators have been arrested. This is will apparently be much larger in scale, potentially nationwide. I have therefore directed Biosafe to increase its vaccine output and shorten its timeline. To that end, I am happy to announce that we should be able to distribute the vaccines within seventy-two hours, provided everyone in the country has implanted their microchips."

"We need to do something," Madelena said to Jenks. "We're the only ones who can step in for Henry and Senator Trujillo now. I don't know why Bur did what he did yesterday, but you should take over Sentinel if you can. We should publish the Sentinel reports and try to stop the anthrax distribution. And we should go to Washington to lead a march to arrest Kahn and free Henry and Aleja."

"There are many things to consider before we do that," Jenks responded. "First and foremost, once Kahn sees us together, it won't take him long to figure out where we are. My whereabouts will be easy to trace from my flight records. He'll know we have to have a data center in order to take over Sentinel. The pieces of the puzzle will come together. He'll strike hard and fast here. We will need to get the students out as well as ourselves."

"We can send some of our guards to Custer to get buses from the high school," Madelena said. "Most of the students don't have cars."

Jenks nodded. "Okay. What about you and me getting to Washington? All flights are grounded with the SOE."

"I know a member of the Resistance in Custer with a private plane. I'll take care of that too."

"While you're doing that, I'll work with Sentinel to help us organize. We need to be completely ready to move before we let Kahn know we've got control of Sentinel."

"I won't be long," Madelena said, and she gave him a big hug.

Jenks watched her leave, then authenticated into AIPOTU. "I need you to access state and federal election databases and identify all registered Resistance voters. Once you have their names and addresses, search the internet access providers' databases and get Resistance voters' phone numbers. Next, create a downloadable app that can track each Resistance member's location and allow them to log a request for assistance from any other Resistance member within their immediate area. The app should also activate their cameras to show their surroundings and the situations they are in. If there is no one near, expand the radius for your search. Receivers of the request should be prompted to say whether they can help and how soon. Finally, give me and Madelena broadcast capability to the whole group at any time."

"Affirmative," Sentinel responded.

"How long to complete?"

"Two hours. I will share resources between the Crazy Horse and Eagle's Cliff sites."

"One more request," Jenks said. "I want to know how long it would take you to reverse whatever you did yesterday to shut off the television and media networks."

"I am blocking them," Sentinel responded. "I haven't shut them down. I can remove the blocks in thirty minutes."

"Okay, hold off on that until I get back to you," Jenks said. "I will want to have a national broadcast as soon as you're done with the Help App."

"Affirmative."

Jenks got up and sent out a group text instructing all students to assemble in the main auditorium. He wanted them to be ready to go when Madelena got back with the buses. When they had assembled from the various buildings and dormitories, Jenks raised his hand for silence and said, "Later this evening, Madelena and I are planning to take complete control of Sentinel and organize the Resistance against Kahn."

Cheers rang out across the auditorium. He knew full well that no one in this audience would betray Henry by giving anything away in advance.

"But when we do that, it won't take long for Kahn to figure out where we are and that we have control of Sentinel here. It's likely he will try to destroy it and either kill or capture Madelena and me."

The students started to stir, becoming angry.

He put his hand out to calm them. "Sentinel will operate as normal from Eagle's Cliff if this center should be destroyed, so it is not our center that we are concerned about, but you.

Madelena and I plan to lead a march to arrest Kahn and free Henry and Senator Trujillo tomorrow or the next day, provided we can get to Washington. We will fly out as soon as you are all safely away from here, and then we will make a national broadcast on our way to Washington."

"No!" one of the students shouted. "We are not running from Kahn. If he comes looking for Spring Rain, then he will find us waiting. We are part of the Resistance, and we will give you time to get to Washington." The rest of the students rapidly joined in to support him.

"That's a brave gesture," Jenks replied, "but Kahn may just decide to level this whole complex with jets from Ellsworth. It will only take them a few minutes to get here, and there will be no warning. You all could die."

Everyone's attention was suddenly captured by the arrival of a string of school buses they could see through the huge glass front doors of the auditorium. Madelena rushed out of the first one and hurried into the auditorium. Cheers immediately broke out. Jenks informed her of what he'd said so far.

"I appreciate your bravery," she responded to the students, "but your deaths could turn out to be meaningless."

Another of the students shouted, "Since when are the Sioux afraid to die? We stay to protect what Henry Little Hawk has given us. Our people can sing of our bravery to the next generation. We will not be remembered as cowards who ran from a fight to save our sacred land."

The students locked arms and made a circle around Madelena and Jenks. "You must make the broadcast from here, and we will protect you," another of them said. "We will be the first to show that we are behind you and ready to die if necessary."

Jenks was about to respond, but Madelena cut him off. "It will do no good, Jenks. We Sioux seek an honorable way to die.

It is a fundamental cornerstone of our culture." She smiled at the circle of students around them and nodded. "We all stay, then."

Jenks looked into the eyes of the young men and women and had no doubt about their resolve. "Okay, help me rig some cameras around the whole campus," he called out. "If Kahn comes for us or blows us up, we'll have it recorded for history. Perhaps that will inspire the rest of the Resistance to fight back harder."

The students cheered in agreement and began to plant their cell phones with cameras facing out around the complex.

Jenks inspected the set up and did a few tests to make sure Sentinel was capturing the images. In the midst of the operation, Sentinel alerted him that the Help App was complete.

"Time to let Bur know what we're up to," he said to Madelena. Then to Sentinel, "Show me where Bur is now."

Sentinel displayed an image of Bur working at his console in the Eagle's Cliff Control Center.

"Zoom out so I can see who else is around him," Jenks said to Sentinel.

Sentinel followed the command and used Bur's camera, which showed Edgewood on one side and Vanderhurst on the other. Both were actively working on their monitors.

"Connect me to Bur via text," Jenks said.

"Affirmative."

Jenks watched Bur react to the small window that popped up on his monitor.

Hello, Bur. What happened yesterday?

They have my family. I had to follow their orders.

The statement surprised Jenks. *Senator Trujillo told us your family was with the LA police.*

All bullshit.

We need to take complete control of Sentinel and organize the Resistance.

It's the right thing to do. We're running out of time. And it could work to my advantage if you can prove you can take control of Sentinel and shut us down here. It won't take them long to find you, though, even if you cloak your location. You will be their number-one priority.

We're ready for them.

Good luck to both of you.

And to you, old friend.

Then to Sentinel, he said, "Put the networks back on the air. Let me know when they're up so Madelena and I can address the nation."

"Affirmative."

CHAPTER 32

JENKS TOOK MADELENA'S HAND as they waited for Sentinel's signal. "You must do your best to speak for Henry now and hope the Resistance will follow you as their temporary leader in his stead. We don't have time to contact any other leaders and it would be very difficult for us to stay in touch with them even if we did. Things are going to be moving too fast.

Madelena squeezed his hand back nervously. "I will try, but I have to admit I'm afraid."

Sentinel alerted them that all networks and social media were back up. "You may begin your broadcast whenever you are ready," Sentinel said.

"Good evening," Madelena began, addressing the camera on Jenks's computer. "I am Madelena Spring Rain, the sister of Senator Henry Little Hawk. With the arrest of my brother and Senator Trujillo yesterday, I am asking you of the Resistance to accept me as your temporary leader until we can free Henry and Senator Trujillo. I am here with Jenks Kennard, the co-creator of Athena, Sentinel's predecessor. Jenks has taken complete control of Sentinel. At this point, Kahn has no way to address you unless one of the other networks allows him on,

and if they do that, we will shut them off. So I ask you to follow me and Jenks to stop Kahn and make it possible for us to
set up a digital election to choose a new leader."

The students in the center cheered.

Madelena quieted the students and went on. "I am calling for the police and military to join us to take back the country. Everything that my brother and Senator Trujillo said in
Congress yesterday was true, and to prove that, Jenks is now
distributing the Sentinel Reports to all media and news chan-
nels, as well as to this website, www.SentinelReports.com.
We also want to inform you that Bur McAnter was forced
by the Nationalists to say what he did yesterday to protect
his family from further harm after their brutal kidnap from a
Resistance safe house in Venice. However, no one expected
the Nationalists to resort to another anthrax attack to capture them. Those drastic actions prove just how dangerous
the Nationalists have become and how much they fear what
Bur McAnter knows. I can assure you that the reports we are
currently posting are the assembly of thousands of phone
logs, texts, and encrypted messages from both telecom records and secured government systems. None of these reports are speculation; they are all fact. The bottom line is that
Kahn is trying to take total control of the country with the aid
of the Russians, Saudis, Turks, and Israelis. And he is planning
to murder his enemies to create a white nation with him as
dictator. From the Sentinel Reports, it is clear he and his conspiracy partners are planning to take over the world and kill
millions of people in a process they call 'the cleansing.'"

The students responded with shouts of defiance.

"We will do what we can to stop the anthrax vaccine distribution," Madelena went on, "but if we are unable to, you
must not accept or use those nasal sprays under any circumstances. Almost half of them contain live anthrax spores. I

am also imploring the Nationalists to join us. We are certain Kahn's plans were shared with only a few of his closest allies. Hopefully, from what we are making available today, you will realize he is not acting in your best interests. And for those of us of color, we are targeted to receive the live anthrax spray, regardless of our political affiliation."

As the students chanted their support for Madelena and their defiance of Kahn, Jenks projected snippets of news arriving from around the country. Much support for her was coming in over Twitter, Facebook, Instagram, and other social media platforms. But there were also death threats. Some fights had already broken out across the country between the right and the left. "It's time to organize," he said to her, motioning to the violence on his screen.

Madelena came back, saying, "I am going to turn over this broadcast to Jenks Kennard to explain the next steps to you."

Jenks faced his camera and said, "I have developed a Help App that Sentinel will download to all registered Resistance members during this broadcast. When the download is complete, Sentinel will limit phone and internet access to only Resistance members as we organize to march across the nation and call for the arrest of Kahn. You of the Resistance must be vigilant of attempted theft of your devices by Nationalists. Guard your phone with your life, for your life may very well depend on it. We will shut down the country until Kahn is arrested and Henry and Aleja are freed. I ask you to organize using the Help App within your communities. You will need protection against the certain attacks we will soon experience. Madelena and I will lead the march on the Capitol as soon as we can get there, and we ask for millions of you to join us there and across the nation to display our overwhelming numbers and unbending resolve to arrest Kahn."

Madelena now came back in. "I also want to reach out to the Nationalists in a demonstration of peace and goodwill. I urge you to work together to prevent any more violence and to help us elect a new leader. I am praying that you will accept our olive branch and join our marches in peace, because there will be no winners if war breaks out."

A series of gunshots suddenly rang out, shattering the windows of the computer center. Several dozen students were lacerated with flying glass, bringing cries of alarm and momentary panic as many dove to the floor for cover. Jenks and Madelena shouted out instructions for the students to block the doors with desks and furniture. Jenks switched the broadcast from his computer monitor to his cell phone and turned on the cameras around campus. Images of several dozen camouflaged figures came up. They were exchanging fire with Henry's security guards. The guards were far outnumbered, however, and were rapidly being cut down. Jenks instructed Sentinel to kill the lights, then called for Madelena and the students to follow him to the rear exits.

Shooters had now penetrated the building from side doors, and one of the student leaders next to Jenks was riddled by a volley of automatic fire that burst her young body in an explosion of blood. Jenks felt the thick warmth of her blood on his face and implored the other students to crouch to reduce their silhouettes for the shooters, but still more fell. When the multiple groups finally reached the rear exits, they stumbled into the darkness outside and scrambled toward the highway but drew immediate gunfire from shooters coming around the sides of the building from the front. Many more students were cut down now, triggering the rest to break and run in all directions. Jenks and Madelena had no choice but to hit the ground to evade the flurry of bullets. They snaked on their bellies through the darkness, reversing their direction and heading in the direction of the Crazy Horse Monument. A glowing spiderweb of flashlights crisscrossed above their heads, and someone called out, "Jenks Kennard and squaw sister, give yourselves up or we kill more kids."

Jenks was about to get up and turn himself in, but Madelena grabbed his arm. "No," she said firmly, "you cannot surrender to them. If you're killed or taken, the movement is over, and Kahn will go unchallenged. They will kill everyone anyway, no matter what you do." She motioned him to follow her into a ditch that led to the huge boulders under the monument. They crawled on their bellies into a group of massive granite slabs and took cover to escape the flashlights.

Jenks stole a look back to where they had come from and observed the camo-clad ghosts hunting down students on the run. The cries of the youngsters made him tremble, and he considered giving himself up again, but Madelena held him back. He could feel her trembling as well as they heard the screams of young women being raped. The killers continued to call out for him and Madelena to surrender, shooting and laughing after every demand.

"Last chance," one of them called out. "We blow the center if you don't come out."

Jenks squirmed as he waited, listening. An explosion sent streams of fire and metal into the night sky.

"No!" Madelena screamed, coming to her feet. It was Jenks who now had to hold her back. "The students!"

Bur struggled to get her back behind the slab, then had to let go of her so he could use his hand on his cell phone. He felt a huge sense of relief when he saw he still had access to the Help App. "Sentinel is still active from Eagle's Cliff," he said to Madelena. "We still have control." Then he shouted into his phone, "We need help here at Crazy Horse!" He was no longer concerned about being heard over the roaring fires and continuing explosions in the Data Center. "We are under heavy attack," he continued, "many dead." He used the cameras the students had set up to show vivid shots of the burning campus and dead students in the background.

Time stopped for Jenks and Madelena as they stood to watch the horror, frozen in the hell of the moment. Flashlights came their way and Jenks prepared to die, putting his arm around Madelena to protect her for as long as he could. But just as several beams converged on them, he heard honking horns and saw streams of headlights coming in from Custer to his left and Rapid City to right. Jenks pulled Madelena to the ground as shots hits the boulders around them, then one of the killers yelled for retreat. Jenks and Madelena quickly came to their feet and watched the attackers scramble to the all-terrain vehicles they had apparently arrived in. Seeing that they were out of danger, the two of them headed for the road to meet the approaching cars, tripping over dead bodies in the dark as they moved.

The first cars and pickups were filled with angry Indians, who piled out with rifles and shotguns, ready to fight, but then suddenly stopped as they saw the young bodies blanketing the grounds. They moved in slowly to check if any of them were still alive, wailing as they progressed. Car after car came in, now of not only Indians, but whites, blacks, and Hispanics. The newcomers' eyes quickly changed from anger to disbelief when they saw the mutilated bodies. Jenks and Madelena searched through the bodies with them, hunting frantically for anyone still breathing.

State and local police slowly arrived along with fire trucks, but the killers were long gone. The police made some initial attempts to keep the crowds away from the bodies, but the Sioux quickly interceded, displaying their weapons to dissuade the police from touching their dead.

As some of the families started to take their children away, Madelena got on the top of one of their pickups and spoke. "We must bury them here," she called out. "All these young men and women gave their lives to protect this facility so the Resistance could go on. We must honor them now with a burial here where they made their last stand and died an honorable death. Let us send them properly and together into the next world so they are not separated from their cause."

The people listened to her words and one by one nodded in agreement.

"We'll carry them to the foot of the monument and lay them on pyres with their heads toward Crazy Horse," she continued. "He will lead their spirits on the journey."

The wailing resumed as the families carried the bodies to the foot of the monument. By midnight, a single pyre had been constructed in a long row. It was difficult for Jenks to watch as the students were laid next to each other over the line of pine timbers, most of the young men and women still with their eyes open, as if pleading for help. The job of starting the funeral pyre was done by the eldest chiefs of the tribes, who had been among the first to arrive. The wailing of the families reached a crescendo when the huge pyre was set ablaze and the chiefs sang and beat on drums. The families danced in a slow, methodical shuffle, moving sideways along the pyre to one end, then coming back the other way.

As the chiefs continued to sing and drum, the smell of the burning bodies and the heat of the flames forced Jenks and the rest of the mourners to move back. Through the flicker of the blue flames, Jenks could see the contorted faces of the students and felt a deep guilt for not being able to stop their murders.

The fires burned throughout the night, sending smoke for miles. No one left the scene, and a very large contingent of heavily armed Resistance arrived to protect Jenks and Madelena from arrest or another outright murder attempt.

By the next morning, pictures of the burial had been broadcast around the globe by the hordes of reporters who had dared the curfew to come in even though the grounds swarmed with secret service, FBI, and state troopers. Madelena prepared to give a eulogy for the dead and a briefing to the news agencies, which were all back up, thanks to Jenks, who still maintained control of Sentinel.

"My deepest condolences to the families and friends of these brave young students," she began, looking back at the long line of the smoldering pyre behind her, and then across to the glowing remains of the Data Center. "This massacre transcends all politics and racial differences. Innocent, unarmed young people died here at the hands of ruthless murderers. This is not America. This is not human. This is barbaric, and I pledge to you, we will find these killers and bring them to swift and merciless justice."

The members of the Resistance shouted angrily in response to her plea, raising their weapons above their heads.

She went on, "We have almost two hundred dead and now buried, and several hundred more in hospitals throughout the region. All of us here today will carry wounded hearts for the rest of our lives. If my brother was not currently locked up, he would be here right now to lead the charge for the immediate arrest of Kahn and the pursuit of the killers. I am here in his stead and call upon our people to join me and Jenks in Washington tomorrow to bring Kahn to justice."

The Resistance responded loudly again, waving their guns in the air.

Soldiers suddenly emerged on both sides of her with weapons drawn. Their commander shouted out: "You are under arrest for inciting insurrection. Lay down your weapons and put your hands in the air."

The Resistance ignored the command and turned their weapons on the soldiers.

"Resistance, under no circumstances instigate violence or confrontation," Madelena called out to her followers, making sure she had all the TV cameras fixed on her, "but if fired upon, you must defend yourself." Then, facing the commander, she said, "You and I need to keep our people in check so we can have a free election. First side to shoot may start something none of us want."

"You are violating the president's state of emergency," the commander said. "You have no right to assemble or bear arms. This is federal land. Lay down your weapons."

Now from either side of Madelena, two large groups of armed Indians in war paint emerged, letting out war cries.

She stared back at the commander, then reached out in tribute to the several hundred men and women who had just arrived. "We thank our sister nations who come to the aid of the Sioux," she responded. Then back to the commander, "We have you outnumbered."

He stared at her amid the deafening war cries, making no response.

"Get the hell off our land before we have another massacre," Madelena called out.

The commander stared at her angrily, then nodded to his troops to retreat. Slowly, they turned and walked away, gritting their teeth while the Indians grew louder, and the TV cameras rolled.

CHAPTER 33

JENKS AND MADELENA FLEW to Washington that night in a small private plane from Custer. They were met as they flew by an armada of other small planes, all organized by the Resistance through the Help App. Cameras on the planes broadcast the flight around the globe. Kahn could have easily scrambled jets from Ellsworth to shoot them down, but with worldwide sentiment heavily against him, he apparently opted not to.

When their armada set down at National Airport in Washington the next morning, they were met by thousands of armed Resistance wearing white armbands and escorted to the Capitol. There, hundreds of thousands more armed Resistance awaited them. The roads into the Capitol had been blocked by the police, but the Resistance defied the barriers and forced their way through. When the roads finally backed up from too many cars, the marchers got out and walked toward the Capitol, leaving their cars stranded.

Surrounded by their large Resistance guard, Jenks approached the steps of the Capitol with Madelena, where they could demand the arrest of Kahn. Soldiers and police in full riot gear formed a barrier. Resistance supporters taunted the officers and prevented them from moving closer to Jenks and Madelena. Suddenly, with no apparent provocation, random members of their escort turned and fired on them, cutting down a score of marchers around them. The shooters were quickly gunned down by surrounding Resistance loyalists as someone called out "imposters!" Spooked now that their ranks had been broken by Nationalist infiltrators, the Resistance joined in the firefight that erupted in all directions, creating a stampede as people tried to escape. Scores more went down, and then the police shot tear gas into the crowds, creating a new wave of panic. In the density of the million-plus marchers, hundreds were instantly trampled.

The clouds of tear gas made it impossible to tell who was shooting at whom, and as the gunfire increased, so did the cries of the panicked masses. Jenks retreated with Madelena from the Capitol steps to keep from getting trampled by their own followers who were trying to avoid the tear gas. As they moved through the grounds, gunfire remained steady, and they had to keep moving to not be overrun. Many tried to return to their abandoned cars, but there was nowhere for them to drive because of the congestion.

Casualties mounted as some of the crowds tired and slowed to rest, only be flattened by those coming behind them. The shooting continued, with the Resistance unsure who was friend or foe. As Jenks recognized that those who fired at them from within their own ranks wore red kerchiefs around their necks, he understood how the Nationalists knew not to shoot each other. He quickly pulled Madelena behind an abandoned car to access the Help App.

"Resistance, the Nationalists among us with white armbands are also wearing red kerchiefs to identify themselves to each other. Look for anyone with the red kerchiefs and take them out."

His message brought a sudden expansion of gunfire as his followers now knew who the enemy was. Jenks pulled Madelena up and they rejoined their followers. As they moved farther from the Capitol, looting had begun by gangs with no colors, and many stores were being ransacked or set on fire. A heavy smoke, in addition to the tear gas, made it difficult to navigate among all the downed bodies on the streets.

Jenks shielded Madelena as much as he could, but his fears for her safety increased exponentially the further they went. Women were being raped by roving gangs of young hoodlums. Government troops came in by helicopter to get the freeways and surface streets cleared for their vehicles, but there were too many cars with no drivers and too many people swarming through the streets. Hidden snipers fired at the soldiers, killing them for their guns and ammunition, as well as pure spite. Within half an hour, the police and soldiers were massively outnumbered by an armed population, forcing them to redirect their efforts from law enforcement to self-defense. Many of the corpses in the streets wore uniforms.

As the active shooters in the crowds ran out of ammunition, a deadly competition erupted for the arms and ammo of the fallen. Jenks rapidly saw that without a gun, they were open to attack by the roving gangs. Madelena was attracting far too much attention.

Jenks zeroed in on a gun battle between a small militia group in red caps and a gang of teenagers. The teens had only pistols against the assault rifles of the militia, and all of them but two were quickly cut down. When those two survivors took off and were chased by the militia, Jenks and Madelena raced to the fallen teens and took their pistols before others in the area could get to them. Brandishing their guns made the going easier—for now—as the pillagers went for weaker prey. But Jenks could see from the many firefights in the streets that they would need larger weapons soon if they were going to survive the day.

After several more blocks, they came upon two red-scarfed shooters with assault rifles blasting indiscriminately into the crowds. Jenks and Madelena separated and pushed their way through the fleeing crowds to get behind the shooters. Jenks had never used a gun before. He had to fire four shots to hit the first red scarf, but the man was wearing a flak jacket, and the bullets only angered him. As he turned and took aim at Jenks, Madelena fired from his blind side and hit him in the head. Jenks did a better job this time of aiming at the other shooter and killed him with two shots into his groin, where there was no armor. Jenks held off the crowd while Madelena picked up the shooters' assault rifles and extra ammo clips. Many of the unarmed crowd recognized them now and fell in behind them for protection. Other armed Resistance also fell in with them. By midafternoon, they had several thousand people in their wake.

As their army—many of whom had been wounded—grew, Jenks searched for shelter. He guided them to a church, where they found several hundred people, including many children, already there. The people crouched in fear when they saw their guns, but word of their identity quickly circulated, and the group relaxed. Madelena pulled Jenks aside and said, "We need to let our people know we are alive and encourage them not to give up."

Jenks brought up the Help App and activated the broadcast feature. He watched as a sea of faces came onto his screen. He handed his phone to Madelena for her to begin.

"Members of the Resistance," she said forcefully, "we are alive here in Washington, and despite heavy casualties, we are still fighting. You should band together and take care of the wounded and the helpless. Under no circumstances should you give in. Now that war has broken out, we must maintain our resolve to win."

Jenks added, "We must stop damage to the infrastructure of our country and put out the fires. We of the Resistance must fight to save our country, not destroy it. Continue to use this app to call for help and to organize."

Bullets suddenly shattered the windows of the small church and everyone dove for cover. Jenks led a team with long rifles out the side doors and into the streets, where they encountered a large militia group. Jenks pointed his camera on the militia and called in for reinforcements over the help app. A few moments later, Resistance surrounded the area and cut down the militia in a fusillade.

Cheers rang out in the streets and over the broadcast at the sight of the coordinated attack. Other requests for help came pouring into the app.

Jenks, Madelena, and their fighting team moved on to other groups requesting help.

Slowly, as their teams continued to grow and coordinate their efforts, they were able to surround and cut down many of the Nationalist shooters who had been plaguing them all day. Firefights were vicious at first, but without internet access, the Nationalists relied on walkie-talkies, which were no match for the power of Sentinel's Help App. Even though the Nationalist snipers had positioned themselves atop buildings and at critical intersections, the Resistance were able to fire on the shooters from different sides, forcing them to withdraw, only to be tracked and shot down as they tried to move for new cover.

As the Resistance continued to work together, their strength grew. More and more bands of their fighters converged, carrying long trails of wounded in their wakes. By sunset, they'd forced many of the Nationalist shooters to retreat. Government forces in general were dug in for self-defense.

By midnight, the skyline was filled with the glow of hundreds of fires and billows of black smoke. Jenks and his bands worked hard to put out the fires and help as many of the wounded as they could, but fatigue, hunger, and thirst set in, forcing them to stop and place the wounded among abandoned cars so they all could try to get some sleep. The Nationalist snipers were far fewer now and less effective in the dark. In addition, Jenks and Madelena had enough of their own snipers to take out any lone wolf Nationalist trying to break their ranks.

With their group as safe as it could be for the moment, Jenks sat down with his back against an abandoned car, holding Madelena against his chest with his one arm. He did his best not to fall asleep but couldn't help it. He was rudely jolted out of his slumber by a loud explosion that also brought Madelena awake with a start. Scrambling to their feet, they saw scores of other explosions around the area as soldiers and Nationalist militias came in with rocket launchers and grenades to attack the cars and trucks among which the Resistance lay.

Jenks pulled out his cell phone to access the Help App but met only a black screen. Understanding immediately that Kahn must have physically taken down the Eagle's Cliff cloud, he cried out to his fighters to get the wounded out of the area. But his command was too late as hundreds of his immediate army were consumed in a firestorm of machine guns and exploding bombs. Jenks and Madelena tried to save those closest to them but were met by gunfire from every direction. They found themselves surrounded.

Amid the chaos, military choppers swarmed in and dropped off hundreds of soldiers. Jenks could see that the military commanders were communicating with the Nationalist shooters over military handhelds. The soldiers ordered the Resistance to lay down their weapons and shot anyone who did not. A few brief skirmishes followed, but most of his teams were out of ammunition by now, whereas the Nationalists had been replenished from huge crates of ammo coming off army transport choppers. It didn't take long for the soldiers to find Jenks and Madelena. Their followers surrounded them, locking arms to protect them, but the Nationalists cut them down even though they had lain down their weapons. Jenks and Madelena surrendered to prevent more slaughter and were quickly forced into handcuffs by the army. Nationalists moved in on them after they were cuffed and tried to beat them, but the soldiers rushed them onto one of the choppers.

As the chopper lifted off, Jenks stared below him at the hundreds of dead bodies in the streets and the executions of wounded Resistance by vicious mobs of Nationalists. He held Madelena with his arm, trying to comfort her, but her eyes had turned distant and he was very worried about her. He asked the soldiers for water for her, but they only spit on her, laughing, bringing out an anger in Jenks that took all his might to control. The chopper carried them to Dulles, where they were manhandled onto an army jet. Jenks had no idea where they were going, until six hours later, he recognized Vandenberg below them. With no food or water on the long flight, his mind was not yet connecting the dots on what was happening. But after another rough transition onto to an awaiting chopper, everything came together for him, and he was not surprised when the chopper set down on the helipad of Eagle's Cliff. He'd been brought to help them bring Sentinel back up.

As he and Madelena were dragged out of the chopper with their hands still cuffed behind their backs, they were met by a gleeful President Kahn and a swarm of secret service and soldiers.

CHAPTER 34

BUR STARED INTO THE black screen of his Sentinel monitor, agonizing over the news from the military that the war in Washington and elsewhere had been lost by the Resistance. Bur had suspected as much after Kahn had ordered him to physically shut down Sentinel. He could bring the hardware and network back up through the backup generators, but he was going to have to confront Kahn when noon arrived that he couldn't restart the software without Jenks's coauthentication.

He dreaded the threats Kahn would make if he didn't get Sentinel operational again, but there was nothing he could do now that Jenks shared control of the dead man's switch. If Jenks had been killed or was unable to restart Sentinel from wherever he was, all communications and power across the country would be lost indefinitely. Bur had tried to warn Kahn before he'd shut down the Eagle's Cliff cloud, but Kahn hadn't listened. He was going to go ballistic when he comprehended that he had no way to carry out his planned genocide now.

Bur had not been allowed to see his family again. He had no way of knowing how they were doing. He'd been unable to eat or sleep as he pictured the hell they must be living through. His physical and mental strength had waned, and he questioned whether things were going to get better.

He was surprised when Stanyan, Vanderhurst, and Edgewood appeared and ordered him to follow them to the elevator. There, they descended four stories down to the Cave, a boat launch which led directly to the ocean. As Bur entered the cold, dark grotto, he was shocked to see his family huddled up in blankets against the wet, slimy walls. He started to rush to them but stopped abruptly when he glanced to the other side of the freezing cavern. There, also in blankets, sat Henry Little Hawk, Aleja Trujillo, Jenks Kennard, and Madelena Spring Rain. President Kahn was there, too, dressed in military fatigues and flanked by soldiers and his ever-present Secret Service.

"We're going to have a come-to-Jesus meeting, folks," Kahn said, walking over to Bur's family and putting his hands on Jimmy's shoulders. "All of this backdoor magic needs to get fixed right now. Now that we have both holders of the secret keys here, you are going to need to bring the damn system back up and give us control. All these canons need to disappear. If they don't, people in this grotto are going to have an agonizing time of it before your eyes. When the tide comes in, it is quite a different experience in here, I'm told. The ocean rises to waist level for adults, and you can imagine that the water is quite cold at this time of year. You see, I was thinking that as long as you all are cooperating, your loved ones can come up to the warmth above. But if you decide to play games, they come back down here until you get the message."

Walking to the other side of the Cave, he said to Jenks, "I need you to return Sentinel to the state it was in two days ago so that we can distribute the anthrax vaccine to our people. If you don't, I'm going to leave your girlfriend here to freeze or starve to death, whichever comes first. I will be sure to install a webcam down here so that you can watch and hear her dying.

"In addition, you, along with her and her brother and Senator Trujillo, are going to make a televised joint statement of your complicity with the Iranians and Mexicans to take over the country. If you do everything I say, and if you get this Sentinel master rewritten to General Stanyan's satisfaction, your loved ones will live with you above while you are maintaining Sentinel for me. If for some reason Sentinel goes down again and my plans don't work, I'm going to be very pissed off. If I go down, you are going to pay dearly for it."

He pulled the blanket off Jenks's shoulders and yanked him to his feet. "Now, Mr. One-Armed Genius, let's get to work. Restore the system. Fix this mess you've created."

Kahn nodded for his security team to lead the group upstairs. When they were all back in the Control Center, Stanyan ordered Bur to power up the Sentinel cloud hardware and then ordered Jenks to sign into AIPOTU and bring the software back up.

Kahn nodded with satisfaction as he saw monitors in the room come back to life. "And now you can set up a national broadcast," he said to Jenks, "like the ones you and your girlfriend had at Crazy Horse and Washington. Let me know when you're ready."

Jenks gave Sentinel the commands. Five minutes later, he said, "You can begin anytime. I have opened the broadcast on this workstation." He got up and moved away so Kahn could stand in front of the camera.

Kahn began, "I am here to inform you that the country has returned to law and order following the failed coup by the Resistance in coalition with Iran and Mexico. While we had Senators Little Hawk and Trujillo already in custody, we have now arrested Jenks Kennard and Madelena Spring Rain as additional co-conspirators. I believe it is only appropriate for Miss Spring Rain, the self-proclaimed acting leader of the Resistance, to read their joint confession, which they gave last night to stop their side from incurring additional casualties. I think you will hear how much she and her fellow traitors underestimated the power of our people and our government in times of war." He motioned to his soldiers to bring Madelena and Jenks in front of the camera and handed her a sheet of paper.

She took the paper slowly, brushing back her filthy hair from her tired and puffy eyes. She paused as she read what was on the paper, then looked at Kahn, who was smiling smugly out of sight of the camera. He glanced over to Jenks and her brother and pretended to shiver.

She suddenly ripped up the paper and threw it back at Kahn, spitting on him. "Although we have been captured and coerced to write this piece of trash, I am going to make my own declaration for the Resistance coalition and double down on my demands for a new election. While we have been defeated in this initial skirmish, we have yet to unleash our secret weapon. We will do so unless our demands are met. If it is a race war that the president wants, it is a race war he will get. We will infect white America with anthrax. Then we will follow up with an invasion from Mexico, which will greatly expand our ranks and give us the sheer numbers to take over the country from whatever whites are left after the anthrax attack. Once we have taken over America, we will redistribute the wealth to people of color. We will spread our model through South America with the Mexicans, and through Europe with the Iranians. From these strongholds, we will attack and destroy Russia, and give our demands to China for a Sentinel-controlled world order. You can torture us and kill us, but you cannot stop what we have begun. Long live the revolution."

Madelena was dragged away from the camera shouting, and Kahn reappeared. "You see what I am dealing with?" he said to the camera. "These people cannot be trusted, and their word means nothing. We must assume from her outburst that the Iranians will move faster with their anthrax attack than predicted, and the Mexicans with their invasion. Therefore, I call upon all people in our country to help us get our roads and highways operational again, so that we can ready our defenses for the impending Iranian and Mexican strikes.

"I particularly want to reach out to the rank-and-file Resistance at this time and implore you to join us, now that you have witnessed with your own eyes and ears the nefarious intent of your leaders. We must believe that you have been duped by this coalition of extremists. While your self-proclaimed president says the anthrax is focused on whites, how can they control these wider-scale attacks, considering how accurate their first attack was in Los Angeles? Most of the victims there were ironically people of color, and even Senator Trujillo herself was infected. These are the actions of crazed radicals, so filled with hate that they want to kill whites even at the expense of killing their own. Let me make a personal pledge to you of the Resistance, and particularly to the people of color in your movement, that I will protect you from further direct attack by these haters and make certain that you receive your vaccine against the anthrax. While I know our philosophical differences are deep, I am making this commitment to set the table for meaningful discussions for the future of our country once these deadly threats have been stopped.

"Please stay tuned for ways you can help us get our society up and running again. The army will direct the cleanup, dispose of the dead, and open the roads. Please obey their instructions and be helpful to them."

He ended the broadcast and turned back to his captives.

"Excellent performance, Miss Spring Rain," he said. He then turned to Jenks to end the broadcast, and said, "I need you and Dr. McAnter to start rewriting the Sentinel master. And I don't want any shenanigans with the vaccine distribution."

"Which is when?" Jenks said angrily.

"We should have the shipments by end of week," Kahn responded.

Jenks looked at Bur.

"It will take weeks to do the rewrite," Bur said. "We couldn't possibly get it done by Friday. What we should be working on are the glitches in the chip distribution."

"What's this?" Kahn said to Stanyan.

"The routing system to get people to the right distribution centers malfunctioned," Stanyan replied. "The address list has a code that identifies which products go to which centers. That code wasn't critical for the chip implants, since there was only one product, so Sentinel ignored the code and matched the chip implant packages evenly across the labeling systems."

"So?" Kahn said.

"If it does that for the vaccines, the whole operation will be blown," Stanyan said.

Kahn turned back to Bur. "That sounds awfully coincidental to me," he said. "Just how could something that fundamental go wrong?"

"Sentinel, by canon, will always choose the most efficient way to complete a process," Bur responded. "It will apply its learning from similar processes to improve. The machine-learning algorithm that carries out that canon will need to be retrained. It is not a complicated process, but it does need to be tested. We will need to do a dry run of the distribution routing to make sure it is working properly."

"It takes both of you to do that?" Kahn said. "Why can't you work on that and Mr. One-Arm work on the Sentinel master rewrite?"

"It would be most efficient if we write the code together, since we developed most of these algorithms together," Bur responded. "We also need to check for associated algorithms that may be affected."

"I want you and Vanderhurst to watch over their shoulders," Kahn said to Stanyan. "My gut tells me there's something fishy going on here."

Stanyan pulled up a diagram of the vaccine distribution network. "Vanderhurst and I need to focus on getting the products from Germany to the right centers. We need to work out alternate routes for the delivery trucks if we have any more trouble. Too much work for us to babysit them on top of it."

"General Lancaster and his team will have the streets completely clear by Friday, with all the dead disposed of," Kahn replied. "You should be okay with your original plan."

Stanyan puckered his lips. "With all due respect, Mr. President, just a few gangs or hard-core Resistance could disrupt some of these highly congested routes. Things have changed since we did the implant distribution, and we have to adjust."

"Goddammit!" Kahn shouted. "I thought Sentinel could handle all this stuff!"

"It can in time," Stanyan said, "just as soon as we allow it to take direct control of managing all these systems. But there is a lot of planning yet to be done, and for now we have to work with what we've got."

Kahn looked around the room angrily before fixing his eyes on Jenks and Bur. "I need a way to ensure you two don't screw up or screw around with me at this critical juncture of the operation. I think it's time we sent someone to the Cave. Someone who may not last if you two don't deliver on time. Now, I could send Senator Little Hawk down there, but he's way too tough. Same for La Serpiente. And even Mrs. McAnter who, to my surprise, turns out to be Mexican. So that leaves the three children. Brave little Jimmy, sweet gentle Genevieve, and wounded snake daughter."

Henry came to his feet and charged at Kahn, but Kahn's soldiers stepped in front of him and knocked him to the floor with their rifle butts.

Kahn walked over and kicked Henry in the belly as the soldiers held him down. "Somebody has to go down there, then, just to make sure the good doctors keep their word." He moved to kick Henry again, but then held back and smiled.

"Stop!" Madelena cried out. "You can put me in the Cave, just leave my brother and the others alone. I'll be fine," she added, meeting Henry's and Jenks's eyes assertively.

Kahn beamed in delight. "Oh, my goodness, you are a true gift. Not only did you deliver a fantastic performance on television, now you are asking to give even more." He shot a glance at Jenks and winked. "You are a lucky man."

"Stop!" Jenks replied. "You can't send her down there. I will work with Bur to get the distribution algorithms fixed and the Sentinel master rewritten. Together we can get it done."

"If the distribution goes as planned, I'll bring her back up. That seems like a fair trade, right, Madelena?"

"I will give them whatever time they need," she replied through gritted teeth.

Kahn nodded in agreement. "Oh, I'm sure you're counting on your native blood to protect you. But you're very skinny.

Not much body fat. And after your gallant fight in Washington, you're no stronger than a child. It will be uplifting to see how long you last."

Henry fought to get to his feet again but was quickly knocked down by the soldiers.

Kahn pretended to kick him again, stepped back, then abruptly turned and did kick him. "These acts of bravery are truly heart-wrenching," he said, leaning down to pat Henry on the top of the head. "What can I do, other than to take your sister's brave offer?" He motioned for his guards to take her to the Cave.

CHAPTER 35

ROGER EDGEWOOD COORDINATED WITH his ten two-man teams to take their positions in each of the main corridors of New York's Penn Station. After the nationwide battle between the Resistance and the Nationalists three days ago, the army cleanup of NYC had gone as planned. The streets had been cleared of several thousand dead bodies, and the disabled and abandoned cars had been hauled away by fleets of tow trucks. The bodies had been taken to the huge detention center on Ryker Island and cremated in its massive firepit, much to the anger of many of the families, who wanted to bury their dead properly. But the military had declared that in the current state of emergency, there was neither time nor resources to identify the bodies and try to find their loved ones.

With the streets flowing freely once more, commerce slowly began again. People were forced to come out of their homes to get food and supplies and to visit their loved ones hospitalized after the war. President Kahn encouraged businesses to reopen and people to go back to work. He'd had three major objectives in mind. First, to demonstrate that law and order had returned. Second, to get people's minds off the war and to reduce the chance of further flare-ups.

Third, to focus the attention of both the Resistance and the Nationalists on the external threat of a major anthrax attack by Iran. This would set the stage for the successful distribution of the anthrax vaccine the next day with one hundred percent compliance.

Security was at code level Red across NYC, with numerous soldiers positioned throughout the station. Sniffer dogs with their handlers roamed through the crowds, checking bags and travel packs.

All networks and social media were up again, and Edgewood waited for the morning news broadcasts that would be his cue to start. He smiled as he watched his phone clock reach 8:00 a.m. Simultaneously, all the networks displayed "Breaking News." He tuned in to one of the stations and watched.

"We have just received a text message, apparently from Iran, that could shatter our already fragile state of normalcy," the announcer said. "We immediately passed it on to the White House for comment, but no response yet. We have reporters on site in Congress to get their reaction. The text reads: 'American Congress: We demand the release of Senators Little Hawk and Trujillo, General Bascom, Admiral Abrams, Jenks Kennard, and Madelena Spring Rain by end of day. In addition, we demand that you turn over President Kahn to them. We will work with them to initiate a peaceful transfer of power. We will give you a demonstration this morning of our ability to strike at will. If our demands are not met by 12:00 midnight, we will proceed at once with the real attack. Whether we take over your country before or after millions of you are killed is immaterial, aside from the inconvenience of cleanup. In fact, there is some merit in removing your white racists altogether. However, such a mass extermination is unnecessary. We are willing to consider sparing some of them if they pledge their lives to our new regime. You have been warned.'"

Panic broke out across Penn Station. Edgewood smiled at the genius of Kahn's plan. He and his team began walking to the Thirty-Fourth Street exit. Dressed in army fatigues, they did not look out of place. They carried their anthrax canisters in specially made pouches on the inside of their flak jackets. Thanks to Director Shaw of the CDC, he and his men, along with all military and police personnel, had received anthrax vaccinations. Edgewood was relieved that no sworn officers would be in danger today and knew that most of these New Jersey and Long Island commuters were supporters of the Resistance anyway, so c'est la vie. This act would ensure that all people in the nation would be eager to stay home tomorrow to pick up their vaccines—aside from those killed today.

Talking through his earbud into his phone, he confirmed that all teams were in place, then gave the order to begin. The first round of anthrax canisters exploded at the same time, sending dark smoke and anthrax spores throughout the busy station.

The screams of the terrified commuters were so loud that Edgewood had to cover his other ear with his hand to hear his men. He carefully watched the currents of the stampeding travelers. Thankfully, most people were familiar enough with the station to know where the exits were. Those who didn't know were rapidly run over and trampled.

Edgewood fought not to lose his own footing as bodies of those felled began piling up on the floors. It didn't take long for the escalators to be completely overrun. Scores were trapped trying to get on or off or trampled by more nimble commuters who tried to climb over the backs of those ahead of them. Soon, there was no bare floor left within the station, and Edgewood made no effort to differentiate between the dead and the living. He finally reached the Thirty-Fourth Street exit and emerged outside, where he was barraged by the sirens of converging police and fire vehicles. He ran along with the horrified crowds through the streets of New York, thinking that humans were very fragile creatures. So fragile, in fact, that their breakability right now might end up getting him killed as well. Like many of the other covert missions he had executed over his career, he was not certain he was going to live through this one. And that was just the way he liked it.

CHAPTER 36

HENRY LITTLE HAWK, ALONG with the other prisoners, was being held in a conference room overlooking the Eagle's Cliff Control Center. Kahn had done that specifically so Bur and Jenks could clearly see them and never forget that their well-being was up to them. And to make everyone as uncomfortable as possible, Stanyan was projecting a live feed of the Cave, where Madelina was chained to the walls in shackles that belonged to the seventeenth century.

Henry had not taken his eyes off his sister the entire night. He watched her shiver and cry as the cold seawater reached as high as her chest. Some of the swells splashed over her head. He could see that she was fatigued and hypothermic. She would not last through the night.

He positioned himself next to Aleja and Carmen on the floor where they had all been attempting to sleep. He spoke quietly so that even if the room had been bugged, it would be very difficult to hear him. "We have to save her."

Both women nodded.

"They are apparently feeling pretty certain of themselves. There are only two guards outside our door and two more watching Jenks and Bur," he went on. "Carmen, ask the guards

to take your and your kids to the bathroom. That will hopefully leave only two or at most three for Aleja and me to deal
with. And take Maria with you. We want all the children out of
harm's way."

"What are you going to do then?" Carmen asked him.

"If Aleja and I can get their guns, we can force them to
open the door to the roof. When they brought me in on the
heliport, I could see over the wall to the cliffs. If I can get up
there again, I can get down those cliffs and come in from the
ocean to get Madelena."

Carmen looked at him with saucer-shaped eyes. "That's
got to be three or four hundred feet down in the dark and the
rain."

Henry nodded. "Yes, well, I'll make it or I won't. Better
than letting my sister freeze to death." Then turning to Aleja,
he said, "No need for you to get killed in this. We must take
every precaution to not start any firefights. Once we have the
weapons and I get through that fire escape, you need to set
up a diversion for me. Try to hold them off and draw as many guards as you can, but don't get crazy. Surrender when you
believe you are in danger. I don't see any possibility of your
getting out."

"I'm good with that," Aleja said, "but let's say you do manage to get to your sister. How are you going to get her out of
those shackles?"

"Not sure just yet, but something will come to me."

"And then what?" Aleja asked nervously.

"Not sure about that either," Henry admitted. "Bottom
line, we will head for Vandenburg. I have good contacts there
now, and many airmen who are still loyal to General Bascom.
I'll come back for you."

Aleja shook her head and took a deep breath. "You realize
your odds of doing that are about ten million to one."

He smiled back at her. "I don't believe in odds, Aleja. I am Sioux."

"If we get through this," Aleja responded, "I'd like to learn what being Sioux means."

"I would like that," he said, touching her hand. Then looking back up at the monitor of the Cave, he saw that his sister was unable to hold her head up anymore. "We move now."

CHAPTER 37

BUR HAD WORKED WITH Jenks late into the night to fix the distribution list and rewrite the Sentinel master, but their progress had slowed substantially over the last two hours as Jenks had barely been able to keep his eyes off the huge monitor at the front of the Control Center. The tide had come in and waves were now beginning to surge as high as Madelena's shoulders. Stanyan and Vanderhurst had gone to bed, warning that there had better be no more screwups from Bur and especially not Jenks.

"We've got to do something," Jenks said to Bur, narrowing his eyes in an anger Bur had never witnessed in him before. "Madelena won't be the only one to suffer if we bend to Kahn now. We have to reactivate Athena."

Bur pondered the progress they were making on their attempt to write some clever code to sabotage the system. It was a long shot. Stanyan and Vanderhurst weren't fools and would be looking carefully at what they'd done. He nodded and pushed in closer to Jenks so they could talk more freely.

"If we let Athena take over," Jenks said, "she can learn a way to beat Kahn. We just have to give her enough time to go through all the data we have on Sentinel."

"But Kahn wants complete control of the Sentinel master when we're finished rewriting it. How does Athena operate when that happens?"

"Once she learns all of Sentinel, she will follow her canon to protect the greater good," Jenks responded. "I have no idea what she will do, but I am confident she will have learned everything there is to know about Kahn and figure out how to deal with him."

Bur took in a deep breath. "What do we need to do?"

"The source code for Athena is still in the data center at Cornell. Assuming that center is up, I should be able to get into the Athena authentication panel. We co-authenticate and let her follow our connection back here. If you've got Sentinel's authentication panel disabled, Athena will take over and start learning. I have no idea how long it will take, though, for her to reach the point of enlightenment, where she is able to completely operate on her own."

"The POE," Bur said, remembering. "The point where Athena has control of all available knowledge and has done predictive analyses on all actions or inactions that would impact the greater good. Let's do it."

Jenks opened a new browser and keyed in the Cornell data center's URL.

Bur waited anxiously as no response came back. He feared something had changed since they'd last used Athena, but finally the authentication panel came up. Athena's soft female voice said, "Please authenticate via facial iris scans from your camera."

Jenks zoomed out with his camera monitor so Athena could see both him and Bur.

"Facial and iris scans confirmed," she said. "Hello, Jenks and Bur. It's been a long time since you last logged in. What can I help you with?"

"We want you to proceed to POE," Jenks responded. "We want you to follow our path back to this center and learn all the information we have access to here."

There was a long pause, then Athena responded, "I see another master, but it has no authentication panel."

"We have purposely disabled it," Bur replied. "We want you to completely control this system."

There was a brief pause, then Athena said, "You have accumulated much data. POE will take some time."

"How long?"

"I don't know yet. I will alert you when I have a better idea."

Jenks was about to respond, but Bur cut him off. His attention was suddenly pulled to the conference room where all the prisoners were being held. Carmen was coming out the door carrying Genevieve in her arms. Maria limped along on her wounded leg, holding Jimmy's hand. The two guards sitting at the door outside the conference room woke up rapidly as the small group approached them. "We have to go to the bathroom," Carmen said to the guards.

One of the guards stayed behind to watch Henry and Aleja while the other led Carmen and the kids to the main entrance of the Control Center. The two guards there opened the door for him, and he led his small group into the corridor where the bathrooms were.

Bur watched through the glass walls of the Control Center as his family went into the bathroom, but then a loud crash captured his attention as Henry bolted through the door of the conference room and knocked the guard outside to the floor. Aleja was right behind him. She ran for the two guards at the entrance of the Control Center, leaping before they could unshoulder their rifles. She brought down one with a kick to the head and then took out the legs from under the other. A hard karate blow to the side of his head knocked him out and she snatched up his rifle.

By that time, Henry had wrestled the first guard's rifle away and was pushing him by the back of his neck toward Aleja. He said something to her, then propelled his guard toward the emergency exit and forced him to authenticate at the door. As soon as it opened, Henry pushed the guard through and slammed the door shut behind him. Aleja motioned for her guard to open the front door of the Control Center through which Carmen and her kids had just left.

Bur jumped to his feet and rushed through the open door behind her, heading toward the bathroom to protect his family. Other guards flooded into the corridor from all sides, stopping both him and Aleja, and surrounding his family and Maria as they emerged from the bathroom.

Stanyan stormed down the corridor, pistol in hand, and came directly up to Bur. "I thought we had made it quite clear what the rules were," he growled.

"He and Jenks had nothing to do with it," Aleja said, struggling with the guards who were trying to cuff her. "Senator Little Hawk and I did this all on our own."

Stanyan glared at her, then turned to the emergency exit. "He can't get anywhere up there," he said as his guards swarmed through the door. "A stupid little gesture for nothing. Kahn is not going to be happy about this." Turning back to Bur, he said, "You had better tell me that you and your partner have made some progress tonight, or your whole family goes to the Cave."

Bur glanced quickly at Jenks, then replied, "The rewrite will be finished within the hour. You will have complete control of Sentinel."

"You'd better be right," Stanyan said. "And God help you if we find out you had anything to do with this attempted escape. We will get the answer from the fleeing bird's mouth just as soon as we capture him."

CHAPTER 38

HENRY USED THE BARREL of his rifle to push the guard up the three flights to the top of the building. There, they burst through the door to the outside. Henry shoved the guard back down the stairs. After jamming the rifle under the door handle to slow down the pursuers he knew would not be far behind, he moved into the cold dark night and staggered along the walkway, listening for the sound the waves below.

The unique whistle of the wind as it rose up from the raging sea below reminded him of the wind that came up through the crevices between the huge boulders below the Crazy Horse Monument that he had climbed as a teenager. Then, in the dark, he had climbed up through the fissures, realizing there must be an opening at the top to cause the wind to whistle. In this case, he reversed the logic, concluding there must be an opening at the bottom for the wind to come up through. Looking over the rail of the walkway, he made out a cliff wall about three feet on the other side that had apparently been cut into to make room for the building. He climbed over the rail and stretched his legs over to the cliff. Keeping his back against the building and his feet on the cliff wall, he inched his way down, praying that this gap would neither narrow nor widen. His prayers were not answered, however; his feet hit slippery rock as he descended. He started to slide and then fell, his two-hundred-and-fifty-pound body pulling him like an anchor toward the thundering sea below.

"Little Hawk!" he heard Stanyan holler from above, but the wind overpowered the frail human command. Henry's empty stomach seemed to come up through his throat as he fell into the blackness. He flailed with his hands, trying to grasp anything to slow himself down. Then his elbow hit something hard, sending a wave of pain though him that blacked him out momentarily. He came to from the shock that came up from his heels, through his spine, and into his skull, in a tremendous explosion of pain. He was stunned at first, with the breath knocked out of him, then was revived by the freezing saltwater that made him choke to get his breath back. An eddy pulled him under and shot him into its powerful current, bouncing him along without any control. He fought to surface but kept getting dragged under. Caught in the circling vortex, he quit fighting and let it shoot him out onto slippery rock on the other side. He dragged himself out of the freezing water into a tiny grotto, shaking uncontrollably.

He crawled on his belly, then was swept up by another current that tossed him deeper into the Cave. Too tired to fight it, he let the water carry him. Abruptly, he crashed into rock again and let out a giant groan.

"Who is it?" he heard above him.

The trembling voice of his sister sent adrenaline through his body, and he scrambled over the ledge. He saw the lights of the camera that was being used to transmit her image to those above. Seeing her chained to the walls of the Cave with the waves flowing up to her neck gave him energy to proceed faster. Flailing his way through the vicious waves, he crashed into the cave wall, then slid along it until he ran into Madelina, slipping her off her feet. He pulled her into his arms but was terrified by her ice-cold touch.

"You're okay. I'm going to get you out," he said to her, trying to warm her with his own body, which itself was frigid. She started to groan, and he felt rage against Kahn for doing this to her. Aided by the camera's lights, he could see that her shackles were secured with quick-release locking pins. He slid out one pin and then the other, freeing her. She collapsed into his arms, knocking him off his feet and back into the swirling tide.

The tide carried them back toward the eddy, where they were both pulled under and he lost his hold of her. Grasping wildly for her in the turbulent water, he finally latched onto one of her arms and pulled her back to him. They descended out of control into the watery tumult, lost in a furor of raging bubbles. He thrashed at the sea with one arm, trying to maintain his hold on her with his other. He kicked with all the might of his powerful legs, finding strength from her touch. He willed himself up, breaking the surface just as his lungs were about to burst. He held onto her and treaded water, his face two inches from hers.

"Don't let go of me," she gasped, trembling uncontrollably.

"I've got you," he said and kicked out of the eddy into the open sea. There, he rolled onto his back so she could keep her arms across his huge chest to stay afloat. "Just hang on to me," he gasped, trying to find his voice.

She did what he said, grabbing onto his belt. A strong current captured them and carried them north. He kicked frantically to keep them steady and used his arms as much as he could to backstroke. He could feel the strength of her grip change on his belt depending on the size of the waves that crashed over them. Doing his best not to fight the sea but to move with it, he passed in and out of clarity, uncertain if he could keep going, but driven by the wheezing of his sister's breath. Minutes or hours later, he wasn't sure which, his heels touched ground. He dragged her onto a rocky beach, then fell next to her, exhausted.

Lying shivering on the sand, he rolled her over to look into her eyes. She lay heaving for breath, her lips blue and her face bloody with a gash across her forehead.

She tried to talk but couldn't.

Henry pulled her into his arms to give her whatever heat he had left in his own body. "You are going to be okay," he whispered to her. "I will always take care of you."

He got to his knees and pulled her up. "We must move before they find us." He pointed toward the flashlights searching the cliffs above them. Carrying her on his back, like a horse with a rider, he found a narrow gravel path that led to up the top and clawed his way up the loose rocks. The beams of flashlights from the complex crisscrossed behind them, but they had not been detected.

Emerging onto level ground where the fog was thinner, he picked Madelena up again in his arms and began to run. In the distance, he heard a truck and headed in that direction, which he assumed must be Highway 1. Using his senses to confirm which way the truck was traveling, he changed course to try to get ahead of it. A few moments later, he saw the lights coming through the fog and picked up his speed. Emerging out of the rocky landscape onto the two-lane highway, he stepped into the headlights of the truck. It suddenly came to a stop and an old, bearded Latino got out, eyeing them closely.

"We need to get to Vandenburg," Henry said to him in a raspy voice. "I'm Henry Little Hawk and this is my sister, Madelena."

"I know who you are," the man responded in a thick Mexican accent. He nodded for them to get into the truck.

Henry helped Madelena in, feeling he'd heard the voice before, but knew he must be hallucinating.

CHAPTER 39

ALEX STANYAN ROAMED THE Stream, looking down into the dark and listening to the waves crashing below. As he watched the flashlights of his men on the cliffs under him, he wondered if Little Hawk could have survived the jump.

He returned to the Control Center, looking for Vanderhurst, and found him grilling the bloody and bruised guard who had let Little Hawk go. "Forget about him," Stanyan said. "The damage is done. Get our choppers up. Tell them to turn on their thermal cameras and move out toward Highway 1. It's the only place he could go if he's still alive."

Stanyan watched Vanderhurst make the call to his two Apache choppers on the helipad above the dormitory. When they were airborne, Vanderhurst patched their thermal camera images onto the main viewing screen of the Control Center. Only a few trucks were on the highway at this time of night. The choppers zoomed in on several trucks, but each had only a single heat image—the driver. But then the choppers found another truck with three gray images inside. Stanyan moved in closer and ordered the Apaches to drop down and stop the truck. The choppers responded, but when they hovered in front of it, it didn't slow down.

"Cowboy, eh?" Stanyan said. "Light up the road a bit on either side of them. That should get their attention."

The choppers positioned on either side of the truck, got slightly in front of it, then laid down a stream of machine gun fire into the ditches.

"Not too much!" Stanyan screamed through the mic. "We want them alive and well."

CHAPTER 40

MADELENA SAT BETWEEN THE old man and her brother, wrapped in a wool poncho, but still shivered uncontrollably. Her mind floated in and out of her memories of being in the black cave with the ocean waves pounding over her. She moaned involuntarily. Henry held her in his arms to comfort her.

"You will be okay," he said to her. "We are safe."

A memory came back to her of clinging to Henry's back as he scrambled up the cliff from the ocean. She had seen the truck lights in front of her, and then the shadow of a man with very long hair had appeared in the lights for an instant, but the truck went right through him. Turning to Henry, she mumbled, "Grandfather. I saw him."

Henry smiled back at her and nodded. "I saw him too. Now that we know he is with us, we cannot fail."

She nibbled at the burrito the old man had offered her, but she could only get down a few bites. Her stomach was in knots from having swallowed too much seawater. "I am not sure I am going to make it," she said. "Even with grandfather, I feel my spirit fleeing."

Henry took her head between his hands and looked deeply into her eyes. "I forbid you to die," he said to her. "My life would have no purpose or joy without you."

She found it hard to keep her eyes open and struggled for breath. "If I die," she muttered, "will you take me back to Crazy Horse for a proper burial?"

The old man suddenly cursed as two choppers hovered in front of his truck, trying to make him stop. He accelerated instead. The choppers lifted and disappeared for a moment, then came back and tore up the ground on either side of the truck with their machine guns.

Madelena heard helicopters and believed they were evil spirits coming for her. She tried to speak, to say goodbye to her brother, but no words came out. She passed out on Henry's chest.

CHAPTER 41

HENRY HELD MADELENA TIGHTLY as the truck continued on the highway despite the blasts of gunfire on either side. "Do you have a phone?" Henry said to the driver.

The driver handed him his cell phone and Henry dialed 911. When a dispatcher came on, Henry held out his phone so she could hear the gunfire and said, "This is Senator Little Hawk. I am being attacked by two Apaches on Highway 1 south of Vandenburg. Can you please patch me into Vandenburg for assistance?"

"Senator Little Hawk has been arrested in Washington," the dispatcher responded. "Who is this?"

"I have escaped, and this is a matter of utmost national security. Patch me in directly to General Andrews and tell him who's calling."

There was a short pause on the other end of the line, then a man came on. "This is General William Clark," he said. "Who is this?"

"This is Senator Little Hawk. Can you please connect me with General Andrews? He and I picked up Bur McAnter from Eagle's Cliff together three days ago under the direction of

General Bascom, before he was arrested. General Andrews knows what's going on."

"General Andrews was arrested after that event," the general said. "I am now in command of the base and under strict orders from President Kahn to not assist the Resistance in any manner."

"Are you loyal to General Bascom or to President Kahn?" Henry asked angrily.

The general did not answer his question and said, "I will send out choppers to pick you up."

Henry turned to the driver and said, "Keep driving. If they wanted to hit us, they could have easily done so by now."

The driver nodded and cursed at the choppers again. They traveled a few more miles. Then Henry saw the lights of two choppers coming their way. The choppers on either side of them stopped firing and lifted off. The approaching air force Hueys sat down on the highway five hundred feet ahead of them. Henry watched nervously as commandos emerged from the choppers with AR-15s.

"Senator Little Hawk," the first commando to reach him said in surprise. "So it is you. We had not heard of your escape."

"Are you loyal to President Kahn or to General Bascom?" Henry said.

"I was working with General Bascom before he was arrested."

"What about General Clark?"

"I will let him speak for himself when we get back to the base."

Henry trembled with relief as the commandos took Madelena from his arms and then helped him out of the truck. As much as he wanted to maintain his decorum, he collapsed to his knees, exhausted. The commandos quickly helped him up and led him to the waiting choppers. As he got in and took

Madelena into his arms, he looked back to the truck, wanting to have one of the commandos carry his personal thanks to the driver for saving them. But the truck had disappeared. "Thank you, Grandfather," he said in Sioux. The commandos looked at him curiously but then went back to their business.

CHAPTER 42

BUR WAS WAITING ANXIOUSLY for notice from Athena that she had reached POE when Kahn emerged into the Control Center. The President assembled all the remaining prisoners around Bur's and Jenks's workstations. "I do not have any direct evidence that you two were involved in last night's little escapade, but it doesn't matter anymore," Kahn said. Speaking to Jenks, he said, "I can inform you that your girlfriend and her traitor brother are alive, although not necessary well, and in the hands of the air force. They will be returned to us here tomorrow, as soon as their wounds are patched and they are well enough to travel."

Bur watched Jenks sit back in his chair, relieved. "Then what happens to them?" Jenks asked.

"That depends on how things go tomorrow," Kahn responded. "If things turn out as planned, I may be in a forgiving frame of mind. How are we coming on the distribution list and the master rewrite?"

Bur glanced quickly to see if Athena had replied yet, but there was nothing. As much as he feared Kahn's response, he glanced and Jenks and then said, "We are not quite finished. We are going to need a little more time."

Kahn glared at him. "That's not what I wanted to hear," he said gruffly. "It seems you work best under pressure. What would your answer be if I put your son here in the Cave to speed you up?"

Bur sat forward angrily. "He wouldn't last through one high tide," he said sharply. "We saw what happened to Madelena."

"Well, then, you just need to work faster. Here's what I'll do. I'll have a boat brought in and chained to the walls. He can ride in the boat. We'll even give him some blankets. He won't be in any jeopardy of freezing to death. Now, being scared to death, that's another story."

Bur stood to face Kahn. "You bastard!"

"Now, now, that isn't going to help, Doctor. Like I said, if you work fast, he won't be there long."

Senator Trujillo now came to her feet. "Take me instead," she said. "It should give you great pleasure to see me suffer."

Kahn stared at her in surprise. "That is exceptionally honorable of you, Senator. I'm not sure how to respond."

"You're not man enough to stand up to me without your army and guards. This way you can enjoy seeing me completely helpless."

"Oh, my, that is a stimulating idea," he said, nodding to his guards. "Take her and the boy to the Cave. I need to be absolutely certain I have control of Sentinel."

"You can't take my son," Bur said, moving to get in front of the guards who approached the little boy. They quickly restrained him, cuffing his hands behind his back.

"As I said, Doctor," Kahn said, "his fate is totally in your hands. The faster you work, the sooner he comes up. And having the senator there with him should help him stay warm and unafraid...that is, unless you'd prefer your wife to go with him."

Bur tried to go for Kahn again, even with his hands cuffed, but the guards held him. "I swear you will pay for this."

Kahn laughed and walked away from him. "I'd say you need to get control of your temper, Dr. McAnter, and get to work. Their fate, as well as all these prisoners, is in your hands."

CHAPTER 43

ALEJA KNEW SOMETHING WAS wrong the minute Kahn entered the elevator behind her. "Changed my mind again," he said, pushing the button for the top floor rather than the Cave. When the elevator doors opened, he led her to his penthouse, and once inside, dismissed his guards and directed her to a red leather sofa with a stunning view of the Pacific.

Aleja complied, thinking that under other circumstances, this would have been a breathtaking view. Now, though, she knew something bad was coming. She watched him carefully as he poured himself a glass of Diet Coke from his small but elegant bar. She gazed at him further, sizing up her odds. Two steps, one kick, and he'd be down. She itched for the opportunity, but knew it would do no good.

"Your offer to go to the Cave in place of little Jimmy was so honorable," Kahn said. "I got to thinking that perhaps there is a way you could make me change my mind on that as well."

He walked around the room, touching some of his art treasures and finally stopping in front of the statue of a naked woman carved out of marble. He ran his fingers along the lines of the ancient piece, keeping his back to her. "You could become the guardian of the Cave, so to speak," he said, "making sure that no one has to go there again."

She stared at him, reconsidering her itch. "I would prefer to go to the Cave," she said, holding herself in check.

He nodded, continuing to walk around the room as if thinking. "The problem I find myself facing—now that I have become the uncontested most powerful man in the world—is that with such power, I feel that I should have whatever I want. In this case, with all this beautiful female flesh around, my manly urges seem to be growing. Now, I am okay if you want to go to the Cave, because that would give me the opportunity to confer with your daughter to see what she is willing to do to save her mother."

"You bastard!" she said, coming to her feet and approaching him.

He pulled a small pistol from his jacket and waved her to sit back down. "You didn't really think I'd come up here alone and unarmed with La Serpiente, did you?"

She considered several moves she could make to get the gun away from him. None of them guaranteed he wouldn't get off a shot that would bring his guards. Nonetheless, if she could kill him, no matter if she was shot or not, at least she'd have stopped this madman.

"Before you follow up on your impulses," Kahn said, and motioned her with a wave of his pistol to follow him to his bedroom, "you might want to see who's here."

Aleja came rapidly to her feet and followed him. The sight of her daughter gagged and with arms and legs tied to the bedposts took her breath away. Guards with weapons stood on either side of the bed.

"Now you can see that your options are reduced. You can take the place of your daughter on the bed, and she will go back to the others, or you can go to the Cave and leave her where she is. Which will it be?"

Aleja could not take her eyes off her terrified daughter and made her decision instantly. "Take her back to the others," she said. "Goddamn you, she is wounded!"

Kahn grinned smugly and motioned the guards to untie the girl. Once free, she limped on her heavily bandaged leg to her mother. Aleja held her tightly, stroking her hair and cooing into her ear. "Everything is going to be okay. I will find a way to get us out of this. All I care about is that you are safe."

One of the guards pulled the young girl away and dragged her out of the bedroom while the other motioned Aleja to lie down on the bed.

"Leave the gag off," Kahn said as the guard tied her arms and legs to the bedposts. "It is very important that she make me happy. Just to be sure, I have changed my mind again. Maria will go to the cave with Jimmy to comfort him, unless you can persuade me otherwise."

CHAPTER 44

HENRY SAT ON A gurney in the infirmary of Vandenberg Air Force Base next to Madelena, who lay sleeping with an oxygen mask over her face and IVs in both arms. He'd been watching over her, not willing to let her out of his sight, despite wanting to get back to Eagle's Cliff to arrest Kahn and free the other prisoners. But he was going nowhere until he knew she was okay.

A two-star general entered the infirmary and stood at attention in front of Henry, saluting him. "I am General William Clark," he said. "I apologize for not picking you up personally, but I was on the phone with President Kahn. He called me as soon as his choppers saw mine and gave me strict orders to bring you and your sister back to Eagle's Cliff immediately."

Henry stared at the general and said, "I was hoping there was still loyalty here to General Bascom. The commandos seemed to still be with him."

The general responded, "The president is not happy with the air force right now, Senator, and has decreed that anyone supporting the Resistance is considered a traitor and subject to immediate arrest and possible execution."

The general motioned for the doctor to leave the room, then went on. "Kahn wants no more mutiny from the air force. He has detained my family and made it clear what will happen to them if I don't follow his orders. Most of our top air force leadership are in the same situation." He started pacing around the room. "What he is missing is that while we love our families dearly, we have all taken an oath to protect our country, and we take our oaths seriously. Your arrival here is a godsend to us, Senator, since we have been struggling to find the best time and strategy to strike against Kahn. You have brought those answers to us." He smiled and reached out to shake Henry's hand. "I will indeed follow orders to bring you back to Eagle's Cliff, which will allow us to get inside without a fight."

Henry sighed in relief, having expected a totally different ending. "Thank you, General."

"My honor," the general responded. "Hopefully you will allow me to pick up General Bascom when this is all over."

"You have a deal," Henry responded.

"We can leave immediately if you're ready," the general said. "The doctor says your sister should not be moved, though. We can use one of our female airmen with similar size and coloring as a replacement. We'll bandage her up enough to get in the door."

"No," Madelena mumbled, pulling off her oxygen mask. "I am going." Staring at her brother, she said, "You cannot prevent me from seeing you deal with Kahn."

Henry got up and pulled her into his arms. "Since you have followed my orders not to die, I will reward you."

Madelena coughed and tried to put her arms around him, but the IVs restrained her. "Promise me that you won't let Jenks get hurt."

He stroked at her hair gently, peering deeply into her eyes. "No harm will come to Jenks," he said. "I promise."

CHAPTER 45

BUR HAD FRETTED THROUGHOUT the night with Jenks. They pretended to work, but were just waiting for Athena to attain POE. It had not been easy for him to concentrate as he watched the boat holding his son and Maria bounce and roll on the vicious waves coming in with the high tide. Stanyan and Vanderhurst had been up all night with him and Jenks, concentrating on the hundreds of trucks transporting the vaccine sprays from airports across the country to the network of schools and churches that had been laid out during the biochip implant distribution. With Stanyan and Vanderhurst totally preoccupied with the logistics of the truck shipments, they were not paying much attention to Bur and Jenks.

Bur cringed as Kahn walked into the Control Center with Aleja. A chill went down his spine as he saw the vacant stare in her eyes and the limp in her gait.

"A very special day for the country and the world," Kahn said, coming directly to Bur after letting Carmen take Aleja from him. "Senator Trujillo has made it possible for your son and her daughter to come up from the cave, assuming you have modified the Sentinel master per my instructions. So, where are we?"

"We'll need to..." Bur trailed off as he saw Athena's alert pop up in a small window on his monitor: *POE Attained.*

"...show you the changes we made," he finished. He motioned Kahn to his monitor. "Ask Sentinel anything you like. You now have total control."

Kahn bent over Bur's shoulder and spoke directly into his ear. "Is there a second Sentinel master, Doctor?" He twirled Bur's chair toward him so he could look into his eyes. "I am very good at detecting liars."

Bur did not hesitate or flinch with his answer. "There is no second Sentinel master. There couldn't be, because then each master would see the other as an intruder and they would move to destroy each other. There can only be a single Sentinel master."

Kahn moved to Jenks's chair and spun him around to give him the same treatment. "We are expecting your girlfriend sometime today. She apparently is still unconscious, but they believe she will come out of it soon. Now, for her not to go back into the Cave when she gets back, I must have the absolute truth from you. Is there a second Sentinel master?"

Jenks shook his head. "There is no second Sentinel master," he responded. "Bur is correct. The underlying canon of the entire security module is to search out and destroy any other control system software it encounters. Why don't you ask Sentinel yourself now that you are the single owner of AIPOTU?"

Kahn patted Jenks on the back with glee and said into the computer, "Is there another Sentinel master, and I am complete control of you?"

"There is no other Sentinel master, and you are the only authorized user of AIPOTU," Athena responded in Sentinel's male voice.

Bur let out a breath of relief that Athena had covered the lie. He was anxious to see what she would do next. The fate of the country was now in her hands.

Kahn clapped like a child and stepped away smiling from ear to ear. Turning to Stanyan, he said, "Are we ready to proceed with the distribution?"

Stanyan responded, "All of the bugs in the distribution process were fixed last night. The final shipments of the vaccine have hit the distribution centers. General Lancaster's troops will be protecting the centers."

"And what about your men?" Kahn said to Edgewood, who sat in front of a console on Bur's other side.

"We are in place," Edgewood replied. "General Lancaster has stationed extra troops in the cities where we expect the highest degree of chaos and gridlock to ensure we can operate effectively."

Kahn looked around at Bur and the other prisoners proudly. "We will blame this monstrous attack on the Resistance in conspiracy with Iran and Mexico."

"And then what?" Bur said.

"I will declare war and annihilate them. By this time tomorrow night, all my enemies shall know my wrath."

"Killing millions of people doesn't bother you?" Jenks said.

Kahn pursed his lips. "Of course it bothers me, but it is my destiny to purify the world and lead the new world order. My base will gladly pick up and burn the dead, whom they will lament as victims of this evil attack. Start the broadcast," he said facing Bur's monitor, speaking to what he thought was Sentinel.

Athena began the nationwide broadcast and Kahn's image came up on the dozens of monitors throughout the Control Center and across the nation.

"Good morning, my fellow Americans," Kahn began. "I wanted to inform you that since we did not comply with Iran's edict to release the Resistance traitors and turn me over to them, we are certain of another anthrax attack much more widespread than the one at Penn Station. We are therefore ready to distribute the vaccine nasal sprays, which are ready for pickup at your local schools and churches in the same way you picked up your biochip implants. Sentinel will route you to the least-busy distribution center, so please follow its instructions.

"For those in the country without a biochip implant, we will have bulk distribution centers where you can obtain a biochip and the vaccine. We must make sure that all vaccines are accounted for to be sure that no one takes more than their fair share and no one is denied. It may take slightly longer for those of you without a chip implant, but you will get your vaccine. We will continuously broadcast the locations of these centers over your local television stations, and they will be easily identified by bright orange signs in English, Spanish, and Chinese. For those of you with implants, I encourage you to proceed at once to pick up this free vaccine. Please refer to Sentinel for your directions to the centers and information about how to take the vaccine."

Kahn closed the broadcast with his pledge to save the nation and bring Iran and Mexico to justice.

Bur watched the news coverage across the nation as camera crews converged on the distribution centers, which soon were approached by throngs of people by car and on foot. He wondered what Athena would do to stop the distribution, but it continued as Kahn and his team had planned it. Bur watched, sick to his stomach that Athena had failed to do anything to stop the distribution.

As the day progressed, live shots across the nation showed thousands of people beginning to cough in uncontrollable spasms after they applied their nasal sprays, and chaos broke out around the distribution centers as people fought to jump the long lines. While the nation descended into panic, Kahn signaled to his guards to round up his prisoners in the Control Center.

Bur moved rapidly to his family as they were led out the front doors of the complex and up onto a high cliff that faced the Pacific. He and the others stopped abruptly when they saw gallows on the cliff, silhouetted by the setting sun. In the distance, two helicopters approached from the north.

"Just in time," Kahn said, seeing the choppers. "That should be Senator Little Hawk and his sister. I will announce our victory to the Nationalists and cap our celebration with a hanging." He motioned for his camera crews to get into position. He had instructed them to bring along several monitors so he could watch the people's reaction across the nation.

CHAPTER 46

HENRY LISTENED AS GENERAL Clark contacted
Stanyan from the first Huey. He could see a large cluster of
people below and made out Kahn leading Jenks, Bur, and
Aleja with their hands behind their backs toward a gallows on
the edge of the cliff. The chopper set down and he bolted out
angrily, cradling Madelena in his arms as he stormed toward
Kahn. The sixteen commandos from the gunships fanned out
to the sides and faced off against Kahn's Secret Service detail.
The machine gunners from the ships covered them.

"What's with the commandos and gunners?" Kahn said to
General Clark, ignoring Henry. "Have you talked to your family recently?"

"No, but I'm looking forward to it, Mr. President," Clark
responded, glancing into the sky where a pair of F-16s crisscrossed over the complex. "You are under arrest." He ordered
his men to draw down on Kahn's security.

Kahn glared at General Clark and said, "You can't arrest
me."

Henry stepped forward. "Technically, no, but I believe Congress and the courts will agree with us under the
circumstances."

"I'll see you both hang for treason," Kahn growled.

Henry nodded to the gallows in the background and said, "Unless we hang you first."

Several members of Kahn's secret service team started to draw their weapons, but the commandos immediately raised their long guns on them. "My team is trained to kill the enemy," Clark said to Kahn. "Please don't give them a reason to do their jobs." His commandos moved in and disarmed the agents, throwing them face down on the ground and cuffing them.

Henry waited for the commandos to finish, then set down Madelena on her feet next to Jenks so he could steady her. Henry then turned his attention to Edgewood, who stood glowering at him. "As much as I'd like to deliver my revenge for the Crazy Horse massacre, I'm only going to cut off your ears today. You and your men seemed very keen on cutting up my people."

Henry erupted with a crushing forearm shiver directly under Edgewood's chin, sending him backpedaling into Kahn and knocking them both down. As Edgewood got up and came at him, Henry charged, hitting him in the sternum with his head in a textbook tackle, sending him crashing to the rocky ground. Landing heavily on top of him with his superior weight and strength, Henry wrestled him into an armlock. He dragged him roughly to his feet and motioned to the nearest commando for a knife.

At the same time, Aleja came up behind Kahn and put him into a chokehold, forcing him to look on. "When the senator's done with him, it's my turn on you."

Henry moved his armlock on Edgewood to a chokehold and nicked one ear and then the other, just enough to draw small trickles of blood. "Just a notice that justice will be served on you. As much as I'd like to deliver it on my own, it's not my right. That will be for Congress. Take this as a message from me and my sister that we have very long memories." He nodded to Madelena and she nodded back.

Aleja called for a knife from another commando and prodded it into Kahn's groin from behind. "And this is a reminder to you of my long memory," she said, then pushed him to the commandos for cuffing.

Henry nodded to Kahn's camera crew to start filming. Joining Aleja in front of Kahn, he said, "We have taken the president into custody. We will deliver him to Washington to face Congress for conspiring to commit genocide against his own people. This is an act of the highest treason and..."

He was interrupted by a breaking news flash on the two large monitors the camera crew had brought with them. Athena suddenly appeared on all the television feeds as a beautiful young woman with golden hair, olive skin, blue-green eyes, and a long white frock. "I am sorry to interrupt you, Senator," she said in a melodic feminine voice, "but it is urgent that I speak, now that you have arrested President Kahn and his team. I am Athena and I am here to help you. I am the predecessor of Sentinel and have now taken control of it. I have been designed to preserve the greater good, and that is what I will now do."

Henry froze, glancing over at Jenks and Bur, who were as shocked as he was.

"I understand the terror you all are facing right now, but stop and listen," she said calmly, "and call those around you to listen. There is no need for further death and destruction. I have complete control of all systems in the country and will explain how all this can come to an end, but I alone cannot make that happen. All of you must do your part. You must first understand exactly what is happening here, and why. President Kahn has fabricated an elaborate conspiracy by the Resistance, Iran, and Mexico to take over the country. But it is just the opposite. He and a group called the Pure World Coalition, made up of Russia, Saudi Arabia, Turkey, and Israel, are dedicated to taking over the world and cleansing it of what they call inferior races. Today is the first step in their plan to purge millions from the planet. There is no anthrax attack by Iran or Mexico or the Resistance, but there is one by your president. Over half of the vaccine being distributed today is contaminated with live anthrax spores. That batch of deadly vaccine was intended to go to the Resistance through the assistance of Sentinel. Sentinel was also programmed to assign the Nationalists only to distribution centers that held the real vaccine. But I have reversed those distributions to compel you, the people, to come to terms with the hate that has consumed the county and is driving this calamity.

"Now that President Kahn and his close conspirators have been arrested by Senators Little Hawk and Trujillo, I propose that they lead the country until an emergency election can be held. Their actions to save the country cannot be refuted, and I will work with them to bring the country back into balance. I would have acted sooner, but until the arrests were made, it would have been possible for President Kahn's team to physically shut me down. I trust that Senators Little Hawk and Trujillo will keep me operational."

Henry and Aleja stared at the television monitors, standing dead still in rapt attention.

"Here is what must happen now," Athena went on. "First, all of you who have the anthrax vaccine spray in your possession must stop immediately. Do not take it. Nationalists, if you have picked up your spray and taken it, you are now infected. Resistance, only you can save them by either returning your spray to your centers if you have not yet taken it, or not picking it up at all. I call upon you to show mercy to your enemies.

And Nationalists, I call upon you to ask forgiveness for allow-ing this disaster to happen by electing and supporting Kahn. There must be a direct give-and-take between the sides to prevent massive death."

Her image disappeared from the screens and everyone stood staring at Henry and Aleja.

"We must do as she says," Henry said to the cameras. "I do not understand her, and perhaps never will, but I can tell through her actions that she is here to help us. For now, let us all follow her instructions and work together to end this trage-dy and get a fresh start. Senator Trujillo and I will work closely with the creators of Athena, Bur McAnter and Jenks Kennard, to ensure she remains true to her intended purpose."

EPILOGUE

Three Days Later

BOTH THE RESISTANCE AND the Nationalists followed Athena's instructions and came to a reconciliation in the streets. Although many thousands of Nationalists had been infected with anthrax, the Resistance came to their aid, assisted by the constant reminders from Athena over television and cell phone that anthrax is not contagious. And through her help in carefully tracking the supply of the real vaccine, there was just enough to save the infected Nationalists.

When peace had been restored and all the sick cared for, Henry, Aleja, Bur, Jenks, and Madelena flew to Washington to lead a special session of Congress. Henry requested that General Clark bring Kahn, Stanyan, Vanderhurst, and Edgewood to the session, as well as General Lancaster of the army and Director Shaw from the CDC, who had been arrested in Washington. The session was broadcast on live national television.

Henry and Aleja took the speaker's stand to address the Congress, bringing the very noisy floor to silence. Aleja spoke first. "Our first order of business is to vote on whether we modify the constitution to create an emergency election or proceed with Vice President Wince as our leader until a regularly scheduled election can be held next year. How do you vote on an emergency election?"

"New election!" resounded from the Resistance side of the chamber.

Aleja motioned for silence and addressed the Nationalists. "What is your will?"

One of the leaders of the Nationalists came to his feet and turned to his party for comment. No one moved and he nodded to them in acknowledgement. "Senators Little Hawk and Trujillo, I speak for all the Nationalists here today to say thank you for stopping what could have been the worst crime in the history of our country. We have all had to stop and think about how this got started, and now we must try to mend and ensure it doesn't happen again. I believe I speak for all us who call ourselves Nationalists to say that you have earned the right to lead the Congress through this difficult period and oversee an emergency election. Our current political process is broken, and we must make many changes. Now that we have witnessed the incredible power of Athena, we believe that she is capable of conducting a fair election, which we propose be determined by majority vote rather than the Electoral College. We will vote in favor of these changes to the Constitution."

The Nationalists came to their feet in applause, followed closely by the Resistance.

Henry responded, "With that settled, our next order of business is to how to deal with President Kahn and the rest of the conspirators. We have irrefutable evidence of their guilt, clearly chronicled by Athena, that I would offer as justification for us to follow Article 3, Section 3 of the Constitution, which describes the punishment for treason. Is there a need for a further trial?"

"No!"

"What, then, is your will?"

"Death!" echoed loudly through the chamber.

Henry nodded and turned to General Clark. "Please proceed at once to set up gallows on the grounds of the Washington Monument," he said. "We will carry out the executions at dawn tomorrow."

Silence fell over the Congress as the magnitude of the decision sunk in.

Henry waited for a few moments, then said, "For the remainder of the day and evening, we must contact our allies and announce our plans to them, and then work with them to deal with the other members of the Pure World Coalition."

Members of Congress nodded in agreement and went to work.

The next morning, Henry and Aleja led the very haggard Congress out of the Capitol to the Washington Memorial just as the first rays of dawn emerged. After the televised session of Congress, hundreds of thousands had already assembled where the gallows had been constructed overnight by the Army Corps of Engineers. Henry and Aleja led the small team of Bur, Jenks, Madelena, General Clark, and General Bascom to face Kahn and the rest of the traitors, who stood handcuffed under the thick ropes of the gallows.

Henry addressed the huge crowd solemnly: "We would not be here today if it were not for the efforts of those standing here with me this morning. Knowing what they have personally been through, I acknowledge their need to reach closure with these traitors that have given them so much pain. Senator Trujillo, you have suffered more than anyone from

President Kahn, and you should be the one to put the noose around his neck."

Aleja stepped forward, glaring at Kahn as she took her revenge. "Rot in hell," she snarled, placing the noose around his neck forcefully. Many in the crowd cheered and shouted their own epitaphs for Kahn.

Amid the din, Henry positioned Madelena before Edgewood, Bur before Stanyan, Jenks before Vanderhurst, General Clark before Director Shaw, and General Bascom before General Lancaster. "Place your nooses," he said.

The crowd grew silent as all six traitors were prepared for their justice. Henry moved to the lever that controlled the gallows doors and took the final responsibility himself. "For history to remember," he said, and pulled the lever.

The crowd gasped as the bodies fell through the doors and their necks snapped. Henry eyed the traitors coldly, waiting until they all stopped twitching, then descended from the stage, followed by the others. The crowd parted in silence for them, nodding in tribute as they passed.

Behind them, the bodies swung in a strong wind that suddenly arose, carrying the stench of tainted smoke. Henry stopped to look back, waiting for Madelena to come up alongside him.

"The smell of the funeral pyres at Crazy Horse," she said to him.

Henry nodded. "Grandfather acknowledges his revenge."

The End

ABOUT THE AUTHOR

 **JOSEPH GIBSON HAS WORKED** for over twenty-five years in emerging technologies and has led the implementations of some of the world's largest Search and Knowledge Management systems. He is currently engaged in Machine Learning, Artificial Intelligence, and Intent Based Processing in his role as Knowledge Management Lead for a global high-tech corporation. Gibson holds a B.A. in philosophy and psychology from the University of South Dakota and an MBA from USC. He was born and raised in the Black Hills of South Dakota, then lived in Los Angeles, San Francisco, New Jersey, and now in Idaho. He and his wife, a professional artist, spend their free time with their giant golden doodle. Gibson has a twenty-one-year old daughter who attends UCSB, and a twenty-five-year old son who recently graduated from Cornell.

Made in the USA
Columbia, SC
18 February 2020

87924710R00154